Art: Alan Evans
Story: Alan Evans and Justin Riley
Color Assists: Aaron Daly and Mabel Lim
Coloring: Kay King
Rival Angels created by
Alan Evans

www.RivalAngels.com

Rival Angels Season 3, Volume 2. ISBN 9780982701379.

I0589792

RIVAL ANGELS

Chapter 5

SHINY AND GOLD

"When you've got something to prove,
there's nothing greater than a challenge."
-Terry Bradshaw

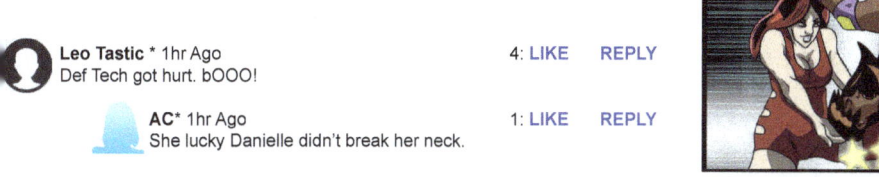

Leo Tastic * 1hr Ago   4: LIKE   REPLY
Def Tech got hurt. bOOO!

> **AC*** 1hr Ago   1: LIKE   REPLY
> She lucky Danielle didn't break her neck.

> > **American Cheese** * 1hr Ago   6: LIKE   REPLY
> > Whatevs. Krystin still ONE.

Chavez Darwint * 2hr Ago   5: LIKE   REPLY
YEES! Yvonne is STILL champion! #StillChamp

> **Zomaya** * 3hr Ago   2: LIKE   REPLY
> Brenda broke that phony champion.

> > **HEY HOW R U** * 1hr Ago   5: LIKE   REPLY
> > Still champ, nut hugger. Yvonne's the champ. Deal with it.

> > > **CEEJ** * 3hr Ago   7: LIKE   REPLY
> > > Until she's fed to Camille.

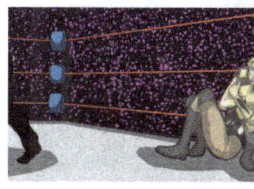

Das* 3hr Ago   9: LIKE   REPLY
ULTRADRAGON WORLD CHAMPS! W00T

> **Under Taker24*** 2hr Ago   1: LIKE   REPLY
> Ultradragon will krak.

> > **Melatonin** * 2hr Ago   8: LIKE   REPLY
> > I see a long title reign.

> > > **GEE MAN** * 3hr Ago   3: LIKE   REPLY
> > > Until they run into Catgirls. #MEOW

GEE MAN * 4hr Ago   5: LIKE   REPLY
Is Gabrielle selling Rival Angels?

> **Zomaya** * 4hr Ago   1: LIKE   REPLY
> SOURCE???

> > **Under Taker24** * 2hr Ago   5: LIKE   REPLY
> > Ur mom

Heated Lime * 5hr Ago   7: LIKE   REPLY
Howabout that Press Conference? Aphrodie and her DD's 0WEND.

> **Tricep Meat** * 3hr Ago   4: LIKE   REPLY
> Until Too Hott told her what's up. #Jobber4liffe

> > **Wedgiesock** * 3hr Ago   6: LIKE   REPLY
> > Camille is FINE.

Season 3
Chapter 3

Art: Alan Evans
Story: Alan Evans and Justin Riley
Color Assists: Aaron Daly and Mabel Lim,
Kay King, Jules Rivera and Dave Reynolds
Rival Angels created by Alan Evans
www.RivalAngels.com

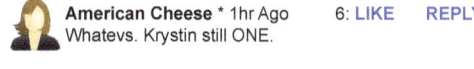

IT'S NOT *JUST* ABOUT WORKING HARD IN THE GYM. IT'S NOT *JUST* DEFENDING THE BELT.

THERE ARE CERTAIN RESPONSIBILITIES THAT COME WITH BEING THE BEST WORLD CHAMPS OF ALL TIME EVER.

THERE'S PROMOTION AND MEDIA OBLIGATIONS. THERE'S RESPONSIBILITIES IN *REPRESENTING* RIVAL ANGELS, AND WE HAVE A STRONG CONNECTION WITH OUR FAN BASE.

WHAT ABOUT THE MAGAZINE COVERS, RED CARPET PARTIES AND TV SHOW GUEST APPEARANCES?

WHAT ABOUT THEM? PEOPLE *LOVE* TO GATHER AROUND A FIRE.

THAT'S THE 'SIZZLE!' THAT WE BRING. PEOPLE LIKE KEEPING UP WITH US BECAUSE THEY KNOW WHERE WE CAME FROM.

WHAT?! SHOUTOUT TO *WRATH AND BODY WORKS*.

SOUTH CAROLINA.

PLANET XTREME.

TENNESSEE IS FOR LOVERS.

JAPAN!

TRIP!
THUNK
GET 'EM!
EEEK!
...
WOW, CEE, THAT LOOKED LIKE A HORRIBLE FALL.
DON'T MOVE.
AFTER ALL THE CRAP YOU'VE PUT ME THROUGH...
I WANT TO REMEMBER YOU JUST LIKE THIS.
KRAK!
OOOOOOHHHHHHH!
LONG LIVE THE REAL QUEEN!
YAAAYY!!

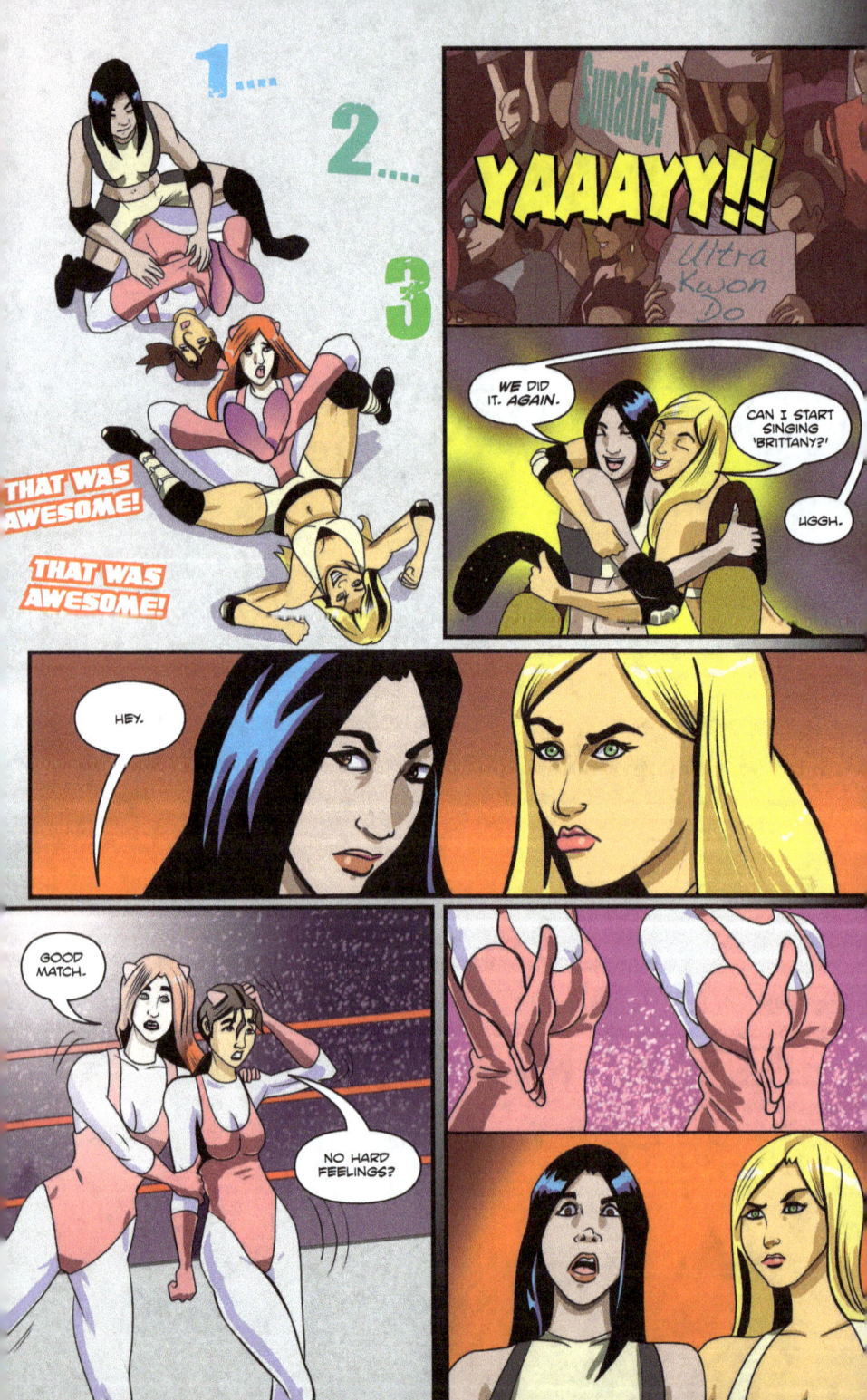

I DON'T *CARE* IF YOU ARE THE TAG CHAMPIONS, YOU DON'T GO INTO BUSINESS FOR *YOURSELVES* BY SHOWING UP UNINVITED TO A COMPETITOR'S SHOW.

SINCE WHEN DID YOU START CARING ABOUT WHAT *BRA* THINKS?

THAT'S NOT THE POINT.

NO MATTER HOW *GREAT* YOU FOUR THINK YOU ARE, YOU'VE BACKED US INTO A CORNER WITHOUT ANY OPTIONS UNLESS WE WANT A LAWSUIT.

WHAT DO THEY WANT?

THEY WANT A JOINT PAY-PER-VIEW.

THAT DOESN'T SOUND SO BAD.

THEY'RE GETTING 60%.

NOT SO GREAT.

WELL, IT'S WHAT I GOT FROM *ATLAS* IN THE *DIVORCE*. I'M SURE THAT'S WHY HE WANTED THAT PERCENTAGE.

YES, I HAVE A LIFE OUTSIDE OF RIVAL ANGELS.

APPARENTLY, I'VE MADE QUESTIONABLE CHOICES, TOO.

SO, WE HAVE TO FIGHT?

NO. YOU HAVE TO WIN.

PFFFT, NO PROBLEM, WE—

RIVAL ANGELS IS THE PINNACLE OF WRESTLING.

WHEN PEOPLE THINK 'WRESTLING,' THEY THINK OF RIVAL ANGELS.

YOU HAVE TO FINISH WHAT YOU STARTED.

THAT MEANS YOU HAVE TO WIN YOUR MATCHES.

OTHERWISE, YOUR ARROGANT LITTLE STUNT WILL SHOW THAT WE ARE, IN FACT, NOT THE BEST IN WRESTLING.

AND THAT WILL NOT BE ACCEPTABLE!

BROOKE, YOU ARE SO MUCH BETTER THAN THAT.

LOOK AT HOW FAR YOU'VE COME!

YOU DON'T NEED A CLOTHES RIPPING *CATFIGHT* TO MAKE PEOPLE RESPECT YOU.

SAID NOBODY EVER.

WELL...WHEN YOU PUT IT LIKE *THAT.*

I'M JUST GOING TO GO FOR IT.

WHAT DO YOU SAY ABOUT MY FIGHTING *MERCY MORRISON* FROM THE MMA ACADEMY AT THIS JOINT PAY-PER-VIEW?

IT'LL CUT INTO BRA'S CUT OF THE REVENUE.

MMA? LIKE IN AN 'OCTAGON?'

YEAH. GLOVES, 5 MINUTE ROUNDS, AND ROUND CARD GIRLS.

ISN'T THAT WHERE FIGHTERS FIGHT ABOUT 3 TIMES A YEAR?

BRENDA FIGHTS MORE THAN *THAT.*

BARELY. SPENDS MORE TIME GETTING TO THE RING THAN BEING IN THE RING.

END chapter 5

Leo Tastic * 1hr Ago   4: LIKE   REPLY
OMG! Upstarts invaded BRA!

> **Das** * 1hr Ago   1: LIKE   REPLY
> Ultragirl got bitch slapped. Hah.

>> **American Cheese** * 1hr Ago   6: LIKE   REPLY
>> Cocoa got busted like a sponge.

Chavez Darwint * 2hr Ago   5: LIKE   REPLY
BRA will end up OWNING Rival Angels after that stunt the Upstarts pulled.

> **Under Taker24** * 3hr Ago   2: LIKE   REPLY
> Like Owning your mA.

>> **GEE MAN** * 1hr Ago   5: LIKE   REPLY
>> Is Gabrielle selling Rival Angels?

AC * 3hr Ago   9: LIKE   REPLY
I hope we see Ozzie vs Brits!

> **Under Taker24** * 2hr Ago   1: LIKE   REPLY
> They should just stay on their own island.

>> **Melatonin** * 2hr Ago   8: LIKE   REPLY
>> Brooke would own. #DD

GEE MAN * 4hr Ago   5: LIKE   REPLY
Cocoa vs Sabrina would be epic. Cocoa is ahead.

> **Zomaya** * 4hr Ago   11: LIKE   REPLY
> They are like peanut butter and chocolate. Yum.

>> **Under Taker24** * 2hr Ago   5: LIKE   REPLY
>> Sabrina got choked out like a noob last time.

>> **Chavez Darwint** * 2hr Ago   8: LIKE   REPLY
>> You're a noob if ou think that happens againt.

Heated Lime * 5hr Ago   7: LIKE   REPLY
Booo! Ultradragon cheated over Catgirls.

> **Tricep Meat** * 3hr Ago   4: LIKE   REPLY
> It was a great match. Epic spots.

Wedgiesock * 5hr Ago   7: LIKE   REPLY
Sun's post fight interview was brilliant. She plays the haters like a fiddle.

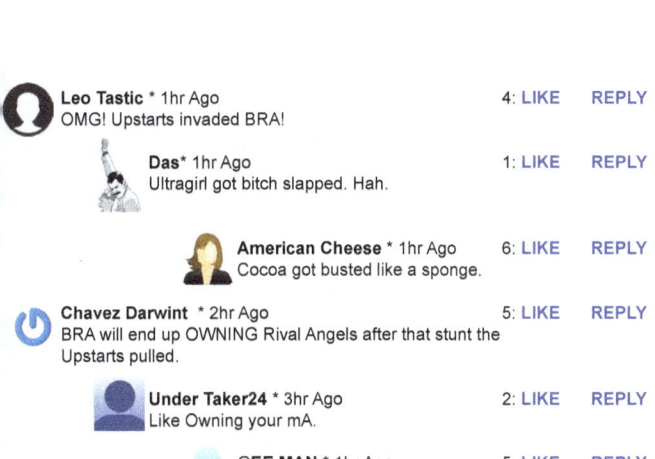

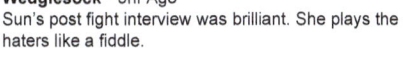

Season 3
Chapter 6

Art: Alan Evans
Story: Alan Evans and Justin Riley
Color Assists: Aaron Daly and Mabel Lim
Colors: Kay King
Rival Angels created by Alan Evans
www.RivalAngels.com

I'LL FIGHT *ANYONE* ON THEIR ROSTER.

YEAH SHE WILL! SHE'LL BEAT THEM TIL THE WHITE MEAT SHOWS!

"DEFEATED? PARTY OF ONE? YOUR ASS WHIPPING IS READY."

WHAT ARE YOU DOING?

I'M BEING YOUR HYPE MAN.

YEP. THAT'S WHAT YOU'RE DOING, ALL RIGHT.

YEAH, I AM.

YOU HEARD ME, 'JUST FOR MEN.'

BRING ANYONE YOU GOT.

NO WAY *I'M* GETTING LEFT OFF THIS PAY-PER-VIEW.

ANYONE?

NOW HOLD ON...

I ACCEPT THE *LITTLE MUNCHKIN'S* CHALLENGE.

A NEW CHALLENGER EMERGES!

GASP!!

FOR GOD'S SAKE, ATLAS. MUST *EVERYTHING* WITH YOU BE SO DRAMATIC?

LISTEN LADIES.

I DON'T NEED TO REMIND YOU THAT WE NEED TO **WIN** THIS PAY-PER-VIEW.

OF COURSE WE WANT TO WIN.

AND YOU PICKED THE **BIGGEST PERSON** ON THEIR ROSTER TO FIGHT?

SHE PICKED **ME!**

AND I DIDN'T BACK DOWN!

WIDOW IS GOING TO PAY FOR UNDER-ESTIMATING ME.

SIGH. WE HAVE NOTHING TO GAIN AND EVERYTHING TO LOSE.

WE ARE **THE BEST** PERIOD.

WE WILL PROVE IT.

YOU GOT IT?

WE GOT IT.

CRYSTAL CLE-

AND FOR THE TIME BEING, DON'T **FRATERNIZE** WITH THE ENEMY.

ER.

WAIT TIL **AFTER** THE PAY-PER-VIEW.

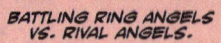

BRAK!

AGH!

YOU'RE GOING TO HAVE TO DO BETTER THAN THAT, KID.

FALL, DAMN YOU!

BLACK WIDOW HAS TAKEN MORE SHOTS THAN A SHOOTING RANGE.

JUST WHEN YOU THINK YOU HAVE HER CORNERED...

YAAAYY!!

FLIP!

SHE MOVES THE CORNER.

CHESTBREAKER!

GAK!

YAAAYY!!

OH MAN, THAT'S JUST NASTY!
WIDOW JUST *PLANTED* SUN THROUGH THE MAT!
THERE'S THAT UNCANNY AGILITY FROM BLACK WIDOW AGAIN.
IF SHE HITS THIS...!
THAT'S *GOTTA* BE *GAME OVER.*
CRUSH!!
GROAN!

THE EARLY WORD IS THAT SUN IS GOING TO BE *OKAY*. SHE WAS *WALKING* UNDER HER OWN POWER.

SHE'LL BE FEELING THE EFFECTS OF THAT *ANCHOR* FALLING ON HER CHEST FOR A FEW *MONTHS*.

COCOA ROCOCO
BRA WORLD CHAMPION

SABRINA MANCINI
RIVAL ANGELS
TAG TEAM CHAMPION

NOW WE HAVE OUR CO-MAIN EVENT FOR THE EVENING.

CO-CO!

CO-CO!

CO-CO!

CO-CO!

COCOA ROCOCO IS DEFINITELY NOT WITHOUT HER FANS AND SUPPORT.

UL-TRA-GIRL

UL-TRA-GIRL

UL-TRA-GIRL

WE'VE WAITED A LONG TIME FOR THIS MATCH.

THE CROWD IS BUZZING IN ANTICIPATION.

HAVE YOU THANKED SUN FOR CARRYING YOU AND THE TAG TITLES?

SUN'S A GOOD FRIEND, NOT LIKE A SERIAL BACKSTABBER...

WHO GOT BOUNCED OUT OF HER OWN COUNTRY FOR BEING A DUPLICITOUS A-HOLE.

MY WAY WORKS!

THAT'S WHY I *DON'T* HAVE A CO-DEPENDANT GROUP BELT.

WHOSE WAY IS BETTER, BRINA?

I DON'T NEED TO SELL OUT MY FRIENDS AND PRINCIPLES TO GET AHEAD.

THAT'S WHY YOU'LL ALWAYS BE *RUA'S* BITCH! CAN'T WIN THE BIG ONE!

TAKE IT *BACK!*

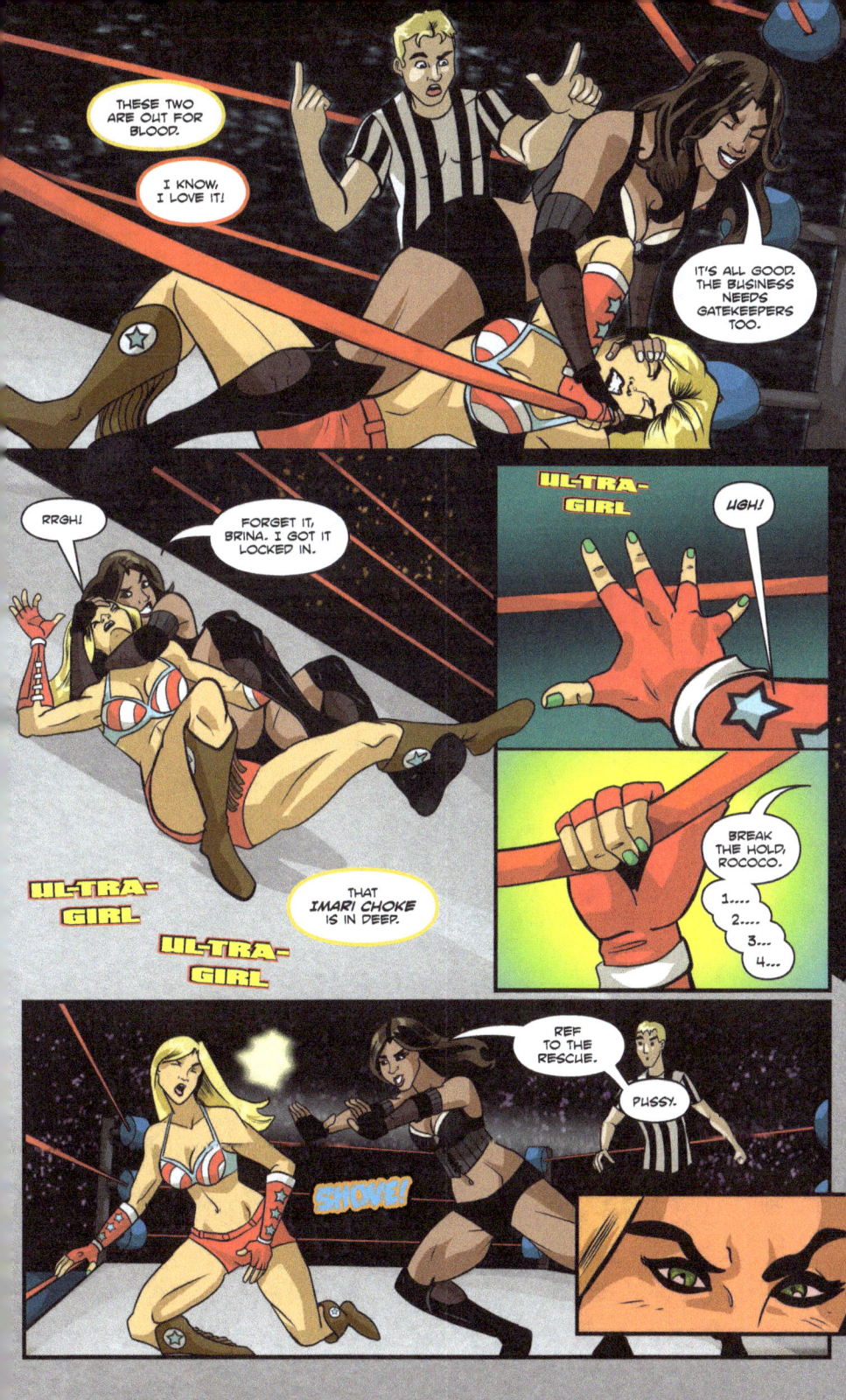

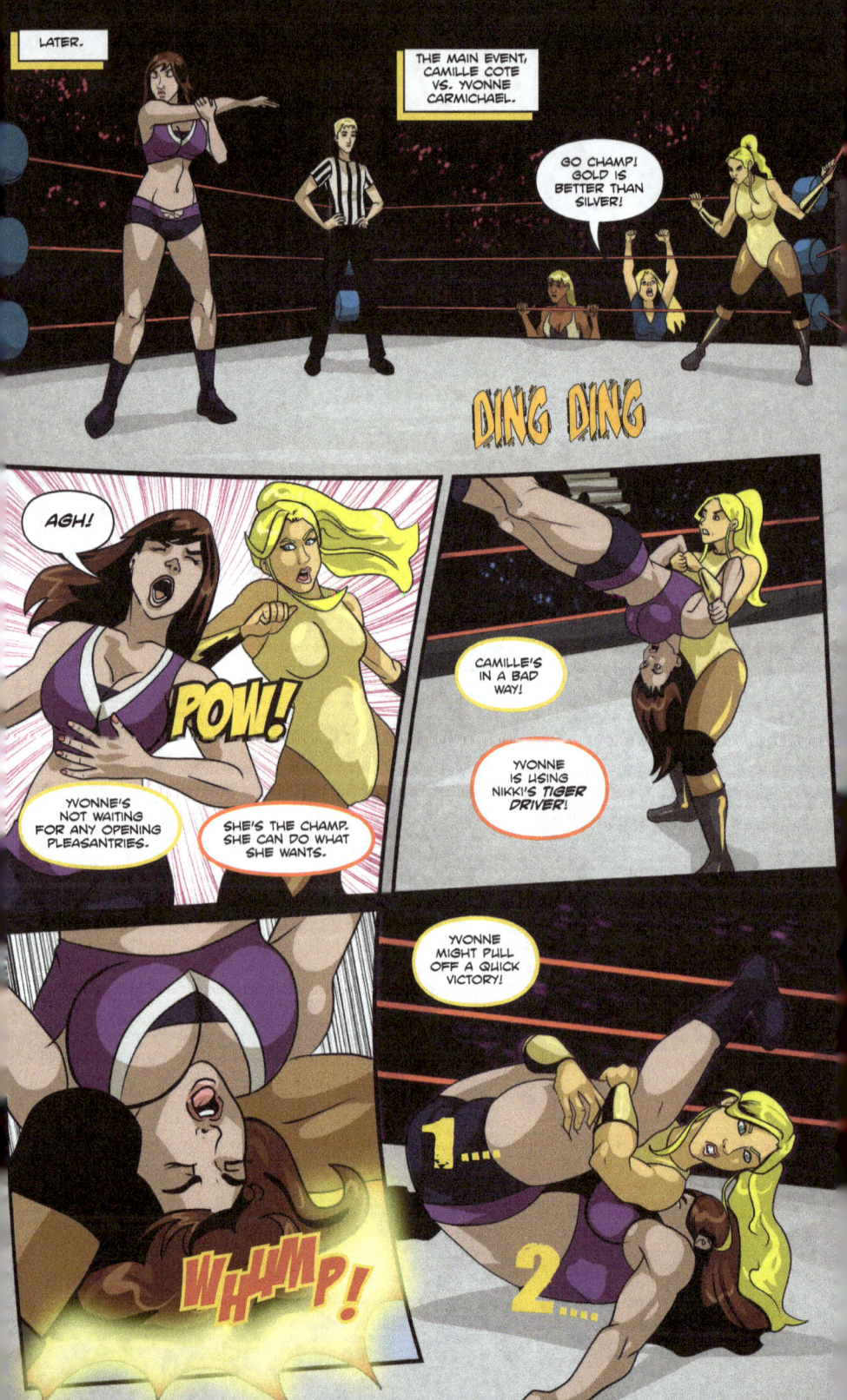

WOW!

CAMILLE KICKED OUT WITH *AUTHORITY*!

THE CHAMP KEEPS HER COMPOSURE AND IS BACK ON THE ATTACK.

THIS HAS GOT TO BE THE MOST DAMAGE WE'VE SEEN CAMILLE EVER TAKE.

ULTRA-KICK?!

LEAVE IT TO YVONNE TO MIX THINGS UP WITH THE HELP OF HER TEAM.

JUST LIKE THAT, THE CHAMPION IS ON THE DEFENSE.

CAMILLE SHOWING GUTS AND RESILIENCY AFTER THAT OPENING FLURRY FROM YVONNE.

BUT YVONNE IS BACK ON TOP, SHOWING WHY *SHE'S* THE CHAMP.

ARGH!

WHAT A SHOT!

AGH!

I THINK CAMILLE TOUCHED HER SPLEEN!

THAT'S IT, *GOLDNIGHT!*

THE 3-COUNT SHOULD BE ACADEMIC.

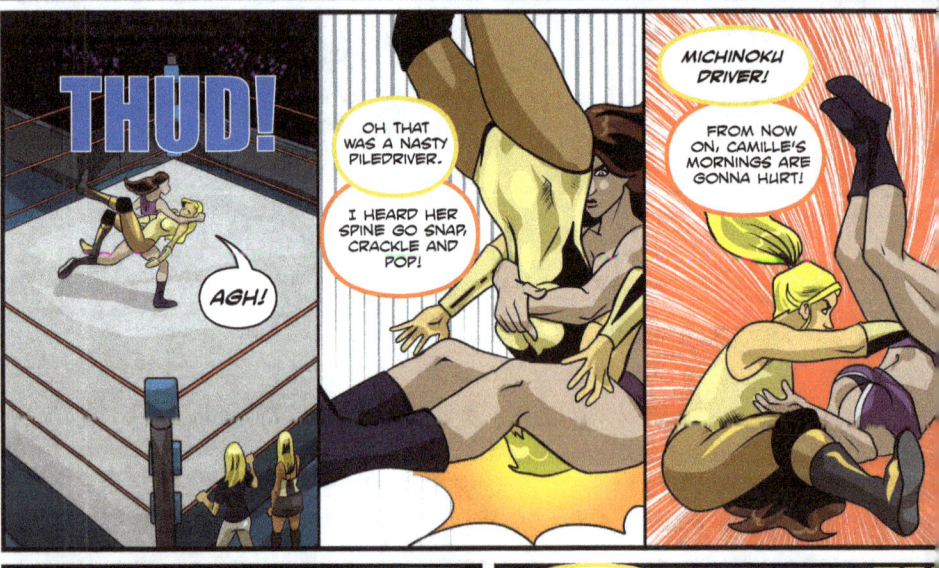

WE CAN TAKE THEM, CAMILLE, RIGHT HERE, RIGHT NOW.

YEAH, NO.

WHAT?

ARE YOU... WORKING...WITH THEM?

WHAT DO YOU THINK, DUMB-DUMB?

TRAITOR!

BLOCK

THAT'S ADORABLE.

WHUMP!

BOOOOOO!

EQUALLY ADORABLE IS YOUR THINKING YOU 'LEVELED UP' TO BE IN THE CHAMPIONSHIP CONVERSATION.

THIS IS THE CLOSEST YOU'LL EVER GET TO THE WORLD CHAMPIONSHIP.

WHAT THE HELL IS GOING ON?

THE WINDS OF CHANGE ARE BLOWING, SWEETIE.

THUD!

GROAN!

IVORY TOWER * 1hr Ago   4: **LIKE**   **REPLY**
3 FATES, WTF??? Rival Angels got 0WNED.

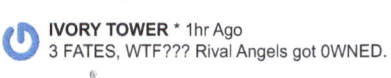

     **OldWrestlingFan*** 1hr Ago   1: **LIKE**   **REPLY**
    Camille, Cocoa and Black Widow are unstoppable.

       Jone Jones * 1hr Ago   6: **LIKE**   **REPLY**
      Is BRA buying Rival Angels?

         Tricep Meat * 3hr Ago   7: **LIKE**   **REPLY**
        That would be SAD!

 **Heated Lime** * 2hr Ago   5: **LIKE**   **REPLY**
Aphrodite looked awesome against jobber Neko.

     Wedgiesock * 3hr Ago   2: **LIKE**   **REPLY**
    The GoDDess brought the glorious win. #goDDess

       Zomaya * 1hr Ago   5: **LIKE**   **REPLY**
      Kaci was terrible to the Goddess.
      Brits are haters of universe.

       CEEJ * 1hr Ago   5: **LIKE**   **REPLY**
      Feed Brenda to Camille.

Leo Tastic: * 2hr Ago   5: **LIKE**   **REPLY**
Anyone ever Sun peeled up from the mat after Black Widow
waffled her?

     Chick Hera * 3hr Ago   2: **LIKE**   **REPLY**
    Of course that was going to happen.
    Black Widow is 10x bigger than Sun..

       Gee Man * 1hr Ago   5: **LIKE**   **REPLY**
      That's what SHE said.

         TIK * 3hr Ago   7: **LIKE**   **REPLY**
        FAIL.

AC * 4hr Ago   5: **LIKE**   **REPLY**
DEF TECH WAS ROBBED!

     OldWrestlingFAn * 4hr Ago   11: **LIKE**   **REPLY**
    MMA is weird.

       Das * 2hr Ago   5: **LIKE**   **REPLY**
      mercy would get owned in pro wrestling.

 Chavez Darwint * 5hr Ago   7: **LIKE**   **REPLY**
Ultragirl took Cocoa, Ho-ho to school!

     Under Taker * 3hr Ago   4: **LIKE**   **REPLY**
    Cocoa> Mancini. #RagDoll

       Das * 2hr Ago   5: **LIKE**   **REPLY**
      Not yesterday with Cocoa flat on her back.

       Imperator Fishrat * 2hr Ago   8: **LIKE**   **REPLY**
      Let's see Ultragirl vs Camille or Brenda!

Season 3
Chapter 7

Art: Alan Evans
Story: Alan Evans and Justin Riley
Color Assists: Aaron Daly and Mabel Lim
Colors: Kay King
Rival Angels created by Alan Evans
www.RivalAngels.com

SHOULD'VE TAKEN THE PIZZA.

2....

RNGH!

3

WE HAVE NEW TAG TEAM CHAMPIONS!

WHAT A HERCULEAN EFFORT BY ULTRADRAGON. IT WAS JUST THE TOWERS OF TERROR'S NIGHT.

THE TOWERS ARE MONSTERS. ULTRADRAGON HAS NOTHING TO BE ASHAMED OF.

APPLAUSE

ULTRADRAGON ★

AGH... MAN...

ARE YOU OKAY, SUN?

I MEAN, OBVIOUSLY WE'RE NOT OKAY, BUT DO YOU WANT TO SEE THE TRAINER...?

I THINK I JUST NEED A MINUTE.

SURE, SUNSHINE. WHATEVER YOU NEED.

IF IT'S A QUESTION OF SPACE...

JAKE, YOU BRING THE COFFEE.

THEN, JUST SAY THE WORD, AND WE CAN GET A PLACE TOGETHER.

CAN I BRING MY *WIFEY*?

OF COURSE.

YOU SAID THAT KINDA FAST.

YOU KNOW WHAT I MEAN.

SABRINA CAN STAY IN THE ROOM OVER THE GARAGE.

JUST LIKE MIKE SEAVER ON *GROWING PAINS*?

I DON'T KNOW WHAT THAT MEANS.

YOU *REALLY* WANT TO DO THIS.

WHAT DO YOU WANT TO DO?

HUH?

CONDO? APARTMENT? HOUSE?

UM...

LOOK, I CAN EXPLAIN THAT PICTURE.

IT'S *NUNYA*.

NONE OF YOUR BUSINESS.

ALL YOU AND THE PEOPLE NEED TO KEEP AN EYE ON IS JUST HOW I *SCHOOL* SABRINA ON SUNDAY.

THERE ARE REPORTS THAT *YOU* ASKED FOR THIS MATCH WITH SABRINA.

DO YOU THINK SHE'S AN EASY TRACK TO THE WORLD TITLE PICTURE AFTER *SHE* LOST THE TAG TITLES JUST A FEW WEEKS AGO?

YOUR WORDS, NOT MINE.

LOOK, SABRINA *IS* TALENTED AND HAS A BRIGHT FUTURE, BUT THE KEY WORD IS, *FUTURE*. LET ME BREAK IT DOWN FOR YOU.

SABRINA IS JUST A LITTLE WANNA-BE OF ME, BUT WITHOUT THE *HAIR, BOOBS* OR *TALENT*.

I CAN'T BELIEVE IT!

WE HAVE A *NEW TV* CHAMPION!

'*BAD BLOOD*' PAY-PER-VIEW, IN PROGRESS.

BLACK WIDOW IS THE TELEVISION CHAMPION IN HER FIRST OFFICIAL MATCH BACK!

SHE *TALKED* HER WAY INTO THE MATCH WITH *VICTORIA* AND IT PAID INSTANT DIVIDENDS.

WITH THIS WIN, THE *THREE FATES* ARE RACKING UP THE *GOLD* IN RIVAL ANGELS AT AN ALARMING RATE.

DOES THIS MEAN THAT COCOA WILL BE JUMPING SHIP FROM BRA TO RIVAL ANGELS?

WILL SHE ACTUALLY SURRENDER HER *BRA WORLD TITLE* TO JOIN RIVAL ANGELS, *DAWN*?

WOULDN'T YOU, *JEFF*? RIVAL ANGELS IS THE PLACE TO BE!

WE'RE GOING TO HAVE TO WAIT ON ANY ANSWERS CONCERNING COCOA, JEFF, BECAUSE WE HAVE THE MAIN EVENT NEXT!

SABRINA 'ULTRAGIRL' MANCINI VS. BRENDA RUA!

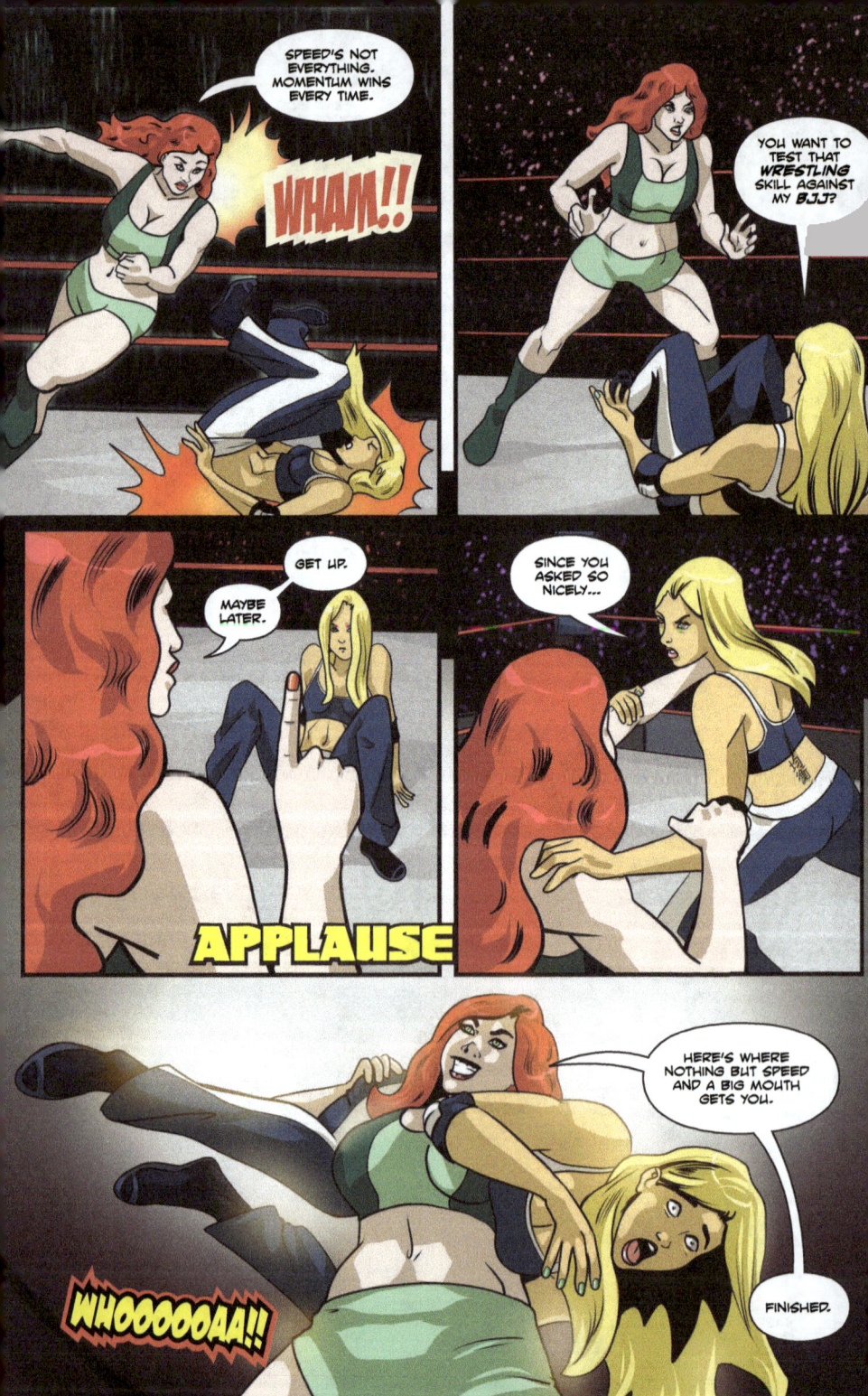

SLAM!

MAYBE *YOU'RE* FINISHED.

I'M JUST GETTING STARTED.

LET'S SEE WHAT YOU GOT THEN.

WILL SABRINA ACTUALLY FOLLOW BRENDA ON TO THE MAT?

SHE'D BE CRAZY TO FALL FOR IT, DAWN.

SABRINA'S GROUND GAME IS INFINITELY IMPROVED, BUT THAT'S NOT HER BAILIWICK.

BAILIWICK?

APPLAUSE

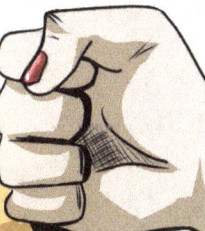

WHAT A GREAT DISPLAY OF SPORTS-MANSHIP.

I GUESS.

WOULD YOU STOP?

BUMP

SPORTS·MAN·SHIP!

SPORTS·MAN·SHIP!

BRENDA'S GOT A DEATH GRIP ON SABRINA.

SQUEEZE

BRAK!

SABRINA'S FIGHTING LIKE HELL, THROWING THOSE HARD ELBOWS.

SABRINA SENSES SHE'S FALLING BEHIND IF SHE DOESN'T MAKE SOMETHING HAPPEN.

SHE'S SHOWING THAT CREATIVE OFFENSE AGAIN.

ANKLE LOCK!

THAT'S THE THING, DAWN. IT'S CREATIVE TO US, BUT BRENDA'S BEEN EVERYWHERE, AND SEEN ALMOST EVERYTHING BEFORE.

AGH!

SABRINA'S HUNG UP LIKE SOME DAMP LAUNDRY.

BRENDA'S CHARGING LIKE A LOCOMOTIVE!

SABRINA CALLS ON THAT CAT LIKE QUICKNESS AGAIN.

RIGHT, BUT SHE'S SEEMINGLY HALF A STEP AWAY FROM CALAMITY.

THUNH

MOVE.
SLAM!
IS SHE TALKING TO BRENDA OR TO US?
I DON'T THINK I WANT TO FIND OUT.
GIVE 'EM HELL.

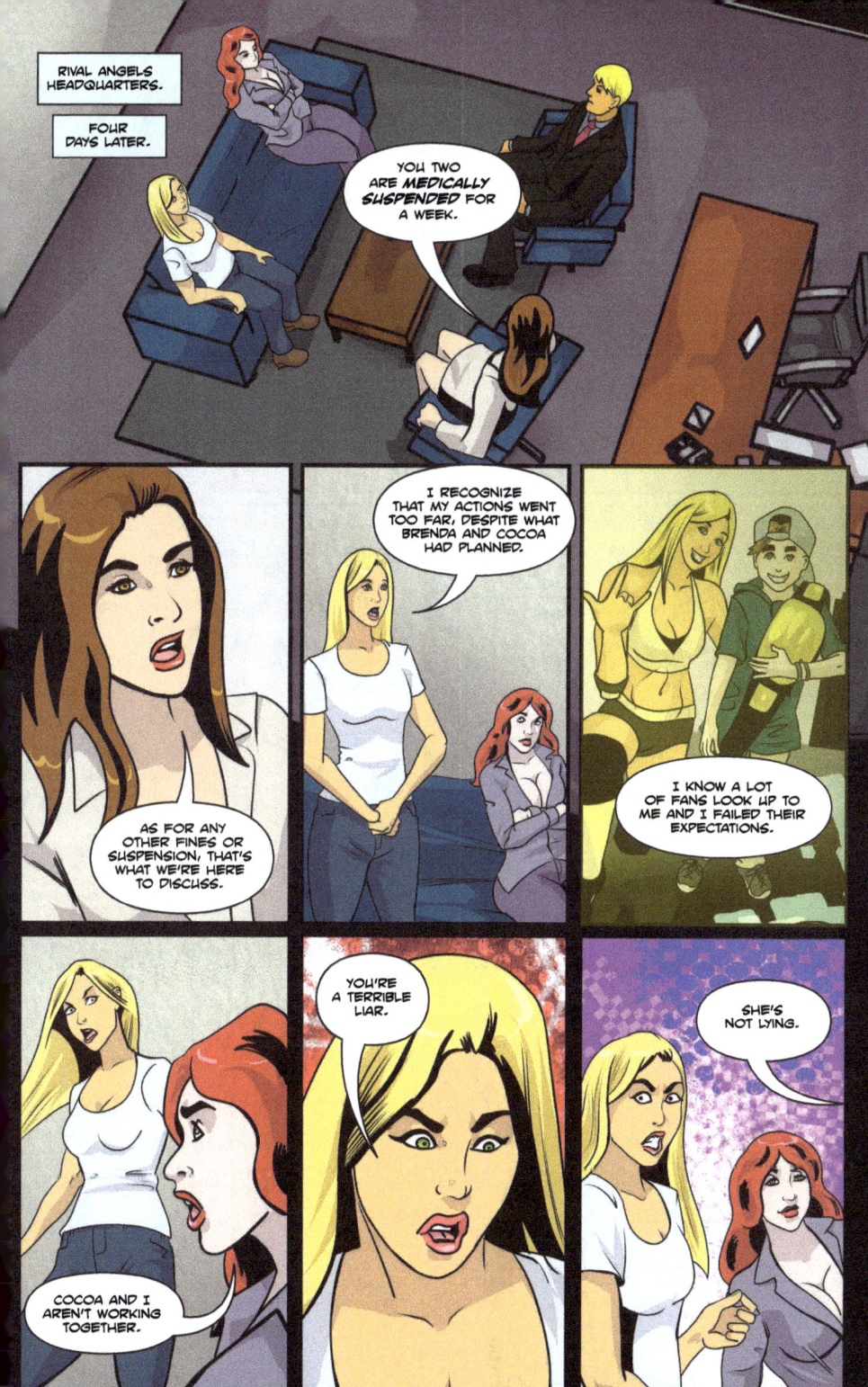

AND EVERYONE SAW ME DROP HER.

BRENDA AND I PUT ON A GREAT MATCH.

AND TO HAVE THAT TAKEN FROM ME BECAUSE OF SOMEONE THAT'S NOT EVEN IN THE *COMPANY* IS WRONG.

I'VE WORKED SO HARD FOR THIS.

EVERYTHING I'VE DONE HAS LED ME HERE.

I'VE SACRIFICED RELATIONSHIPS, SCHOOL, HOBBIES... ALL FOR A *SHOT* AT THE TITLE.

I *BEAT* COCOA.

I *BEAT* BRENDA, REGARDLESS OF WHAT THE RECORD BOOKS SAY.

I *EARNED* THE CHANCE FOR THE WORLD TITLE AT *HEAVEN AND HELL* PAY-PER-VIEW.

WELL, I'M GLAD SHE'S GONE.

TOO MUCH EMOTION IN THE ROOM.

SHOULD WE TALK ABOUT MY TITLE SHOT?

HEY!

IF YOU WANT *RECORD* NUMBERS FOR THE PAY-PER-VIEW, YOU'LL PUT *ME* IN THE TITLE MATCH.

WELL, ACTUALLY–

OH *SHUT UP,* MICHAEL.

I'LL LET YOU KNOW WHAT I DECIDE.

SO...

WHAT DO YOU WANT TO DO?

End chapter 7

RIVAL ANGELS

Chapter 8

' HEAVEN AND HELL' PPV

"It always seems impossible until it's done."
- Nelson Mandela

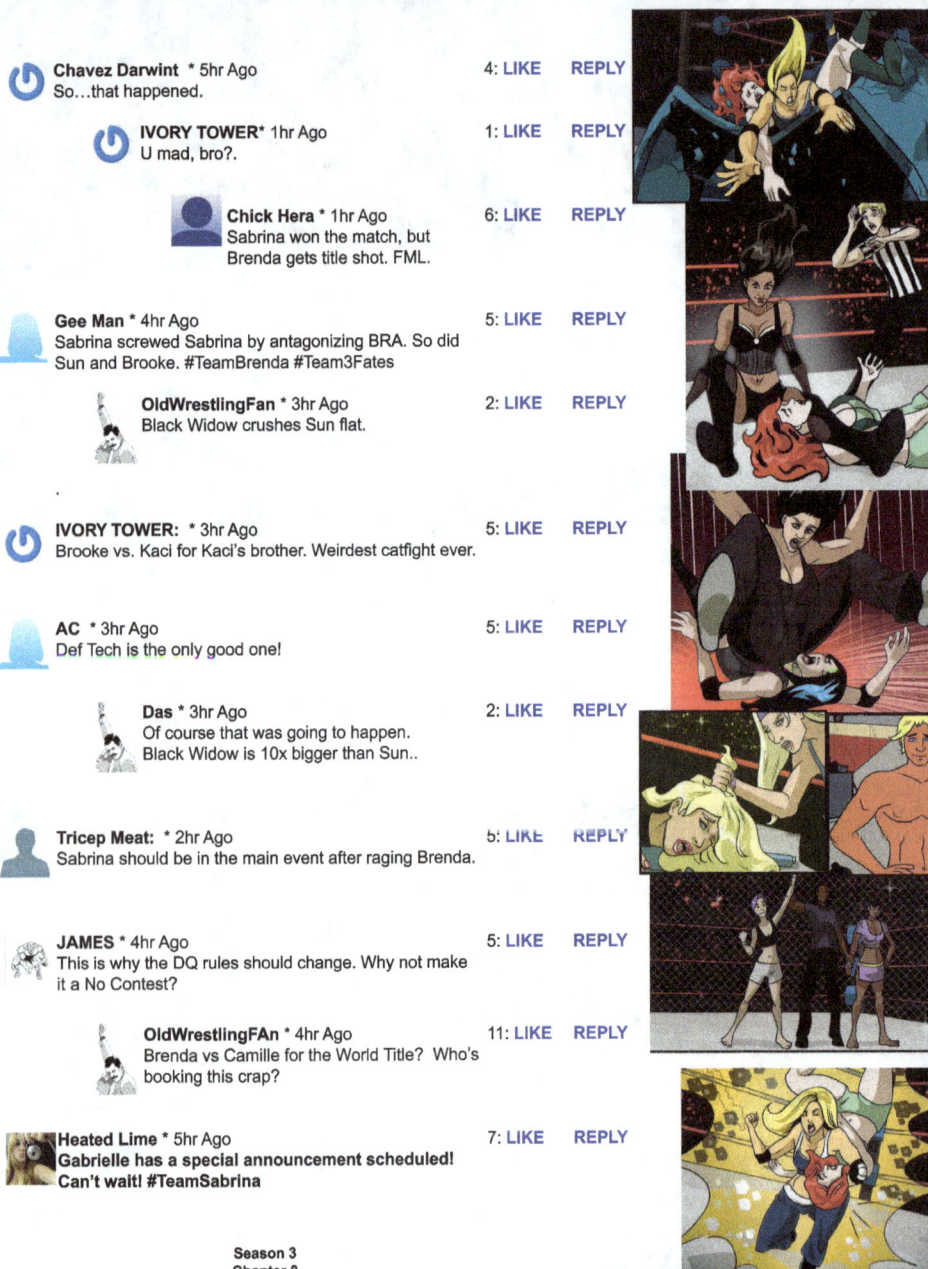

Chavez Darwint * 5hr Ago — 4: LIKE REPLY
So…that happened.

> **IVORY TOWER*** 1hr Ago — 1: LIKE REPLY
> U mad, bro?.

>> **Chick Hera** * 1hr Ago — 6: LIKE REPLY
>> Sabrina won the match, but Brenda gets title shot. FML.

Gee Man * 4hr Ago — 5: LIKE REPLY
Sabrina screwed Sabrina by antagonizing BRA. So did Sun and Brooke. #TeamBrenda #Team3Fates

> **OldWrestlingFan** * 3hr Ago — 2: LIKE REPLY
> Black Widow crushes Sun flat.

IVORY TOWER: * 3hr Ago — 5: LIKE REPLY
Brooke vs. Kaci for Kaci's brother. Weirdest catfight ever.

AC * 3hr Ago — 5: LIKE REPLY
Def Tech is the only good one!

> **Das** * 3hr Ago — 2: LIKE REPLY
> Of course that was going to happen. Black Widow is 10x bigger than Sun..

Tricep Meat: * 2hr Ago — 5: LIKE REPLY
Sabrina should be in the main event after raging Brenda.

JAMES * 4hr Ago — 5: LIKE REPLY
This is why the DQ rules should change. Why not make it a No Contest?

> **OldWrestlingFAn** * 4hr Ago — 11: LIKE REPLY
> Brenda vs Camille for the World Title? Who's booking this crap?

Heated Lime * 5hr Ago — 7: LIKE REPLY
Gabrielle has a special announcement scheduled! Can't wait! #TeamSabrina

Season 3
Chapter 8

Art: Alan Evans
Story: Alan Evans and Justin Riley
Color Assists: Aaron Daly and Mabel Lim
Colors: Kay King
Rival Angels created by Alan Evans

www.RivalAngels.com

UNBELIEVABLE!

THAT IS BLOCKBUSTER NEWS! BUT DOES COCOA ROCOCO REALLY DESERVE TO JUMP THE LINE AHEAD OF A LOT OF CONTENDERS?

COCOA IS THE *BATTLING RING ANGELS* CHAMPION; AND THAT ACCOMPLISH-MENT SPEAKS FOR ITSELF.

HOWEVER, RIVAL ANGELS IS NOT A PART-TIME JOB. IT'S BEEN MADE CLEAR TO COCOA THAT IF SHE WANTS TO COMPETE HERE, SHE MUST *RELINQUISH* HER BRA CHAMPIONSHIP.

WE KNOW THAT COCOA AND CAMILLE ARE THICK AS THIEVES. SHOULD COCOA MAKE IT TO THE MAIN EVENT, WOULDN'T THAT BE UNFAIR TO BRENDA?

COCOA IS KNOWN FOR HER *DUPLICITY* AS MUCH AS HER ACCOMPLISHMENTS.

I'VE NO DOUBT THAT HER *ALLEGIANCE* TO CAMILLE WILL DISSOLVE ONCE SHE REALIZES THAT SHE HAS THE CHANCE TO BECOME THE FIRST EVER TO HOLD BOTH THE BRA WORLD TITLE AND THE COVETED RIVAL ANGELS WORLD TITLE.

IT'S OFFICIAL: THE MAIN EVENT AT HEAVEN AND HELL JUST GOT BIGGER. THE WINNER BETWEEN SABRINA MANCINI AND COCOA ROCOCO MOVES ON TO THE MAIN EVENT FOR THE RIVAL ANGELS WORLD TITLE!

HEAVEN AND HELL PAY-PER-VIEW

MAIN EVENT
WORLD CHAMPIONSHIP
CAMILLE COTE VS. BRENDA RUA VS. ???

CO-MAIN EVENT
TAG TEAM TITLE
TOWERS OF TERROR VS. BLACK AND BLUE

TV CHAMPIONSHIP LADDER MATCH
BLACK WIDOW VS. VICTORIA BUCKINGHAM

APHRODITE VS. KACI ALEXANDER

MMA RULES
KRYSTIN VS. MERCY MORRISON

YORK SISTERS VS. CATGIRLS

RAMPAGE VS. CALLISTA QUINN

DYNA MO VS. DANIELLE PERFECTION

SCHOOLYARD RULES
SUN WONG VS. SARA VALENTINE

LORETTA DIAZ AND PROFESSOR SHANNON MCCOURT VS. KAT SMITH AND JENNIFER NEEDLES

MONICA RUMBLE VS. MISTRESS DARK

LAST WOMAN STANDING
ANGEL SOPRANO VS. SAMMIE SINCLAIR

XTINA CARPENTER VS. AMANDA BREAKER

KYRA GOLD VS. VERONICA SILVER

WINNER GETS ADDED TO MAIN EVENT
SABRINA MANCINI VS. COCOA ROCOCO

CARD SUBJECT TO CHANGE

ANGEL DOME, HOURS BEFORE THE *HEAVEN AND HELL* PAY-PER-VIEW.

RIVAL ANGELS
HEAVEN AND HELL PPV

SNEAK!

ACK!

KRAK!

ARRGH!

KRAK!

KRASH

-MOAN-

HEY, ANDREW.

HEY, SUN!

IS THE DUCHESS IN?

YEAH, GO RIGHT IN.

HERE YOU GO, SABRINA.

THANKS, BRUCE!

SUNSHINE!

HEY, BABY!

HOW ARE YOU SINGLE?

BECAUSE YOU LEFT ME FOR A BOY.

PFFFT. YOU'LL ALWAYS BE MY WIFE.

WHAT UP, BRUCE!

YOU TAKING CARE OF MY GIRL?

AS IF SHE WAS YOU.

THAT'S WHAT I'M TALKING ABOUT.

YOU READY FOR YOUR 'SCHOOLYARD BRAWL' WITH *SARA VALENTINE?*

DOES A BEAR SHIT IN THE POPE'S HAT?

BUT, YOU KNOW...THE CARD IS 'SUBJECT TO CHANGE...'

IS *WONG* IN THERE, ANDREW?

GET OUT OF THE WAY!

IS THAT GABRIELLE?

NOW, SABRINA, DON'T FREAK OUT.

WONG!

WHAT THE HELL...?!

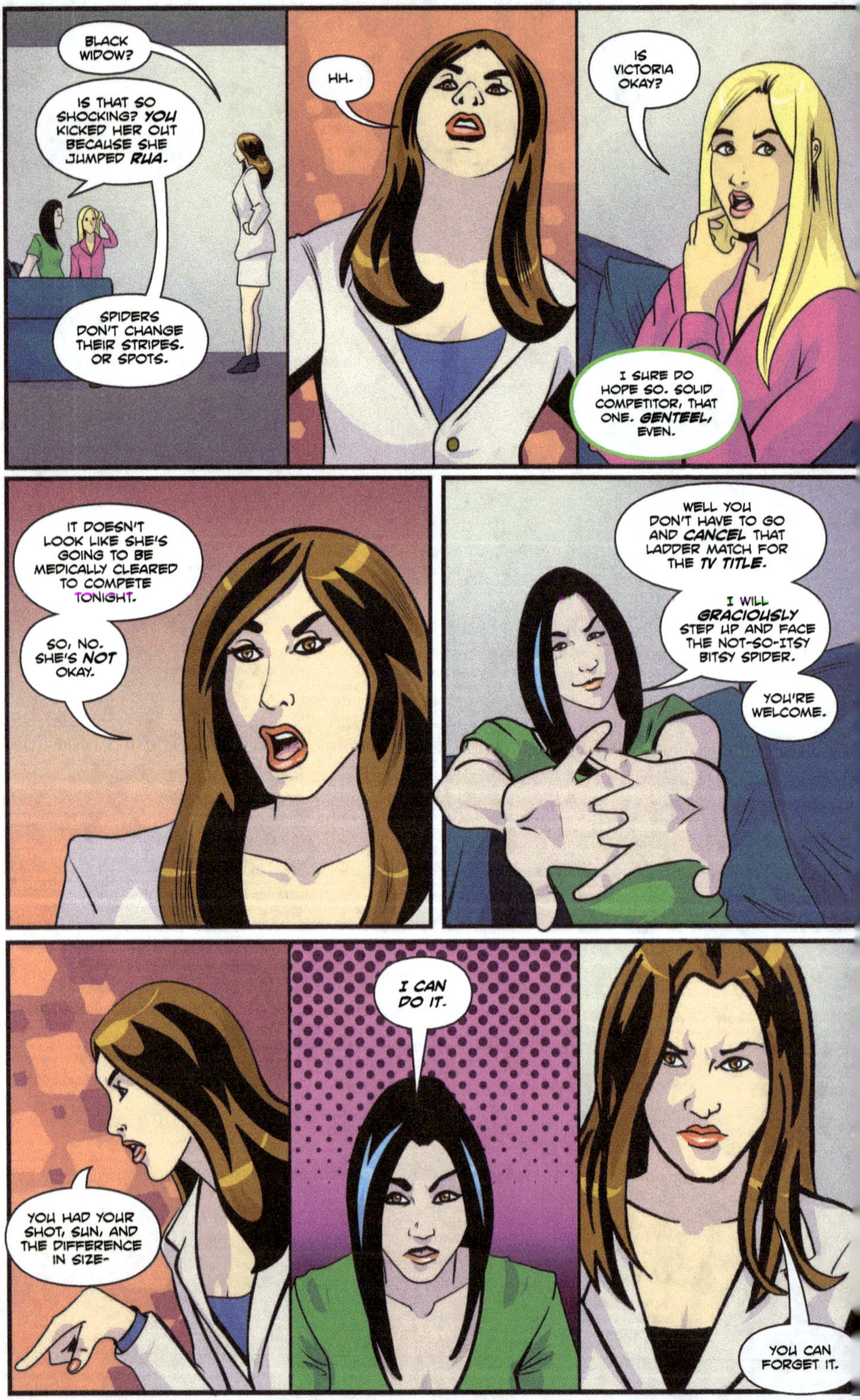

BLACK WIDOW?

IS THAT SO SHOCKING? *YOU* KICKED HER OUT BECAUSE SHE JUMPED *RUA.*

SPIDERS DON'T CHANGE THEIR STRIPES. OR SPOTS.

HH.

IS VICTORIA OKAY?

I SURE DO HOPE SO. SOLID COMPETITOR, THAT ONE. *GENTEEL,* EVEN.

IT DOESN'T LOOK LIKE SHE'S GOING TO BE MEDICALLY CLEARED TO COMPETE TONIGHT.

SO, NO. SHE'S *NOT* OKAY.

WELL YOU DON'T HAVE TO GO AND *CANCEL* THAT LADDER MATCH FOR THE *TV TITLE.*

I WILL *GRACIOUSLY* STEP UP AND FACE THE NOT-SO-ITSY BITSY SPIDER.

YOU'RE WELCOME.

YOU HAD YOUR SHOT, SUN, AND THE DIFFERENCE IN SIZE—

I CAN DO IT.

YOU CAN FORGET IT.

YOU TWO HAVE A LONG WAY TO GO BEFORE YOU CAN MAKE IT 'RIGHT.'

BUT YOU'VE GOT YOUR SHOT, WONG.

DON'T DISAPPOINT ME.

THAT WAS *AMAZING*, BRINA.

THANKS.

I MEANT EVERY WORD, *SUNSHINE.*

SO, DO I *WANT* TO KNOW?

ASK ME NO QUESTIONS AND I'LL TELL YOU NO LIES.

MERCY MORRISON

VS.

KRYSTIN MOLINE

Def Tech

MMA Rules

SUBMISSION, KO OR DECISION AFTER 3 FIVE-MINUTE ROUNDS.

I'M REALLY GLAD YOU'RE HERE, *TOPHER.* NOT JUST AS A COACH, BUT, YOU KNOW...

YEAH.

I'D BE LYING IF I SAID THAT I'D BE HERE WITHOUT *MERCY'S* INSISTENCE THAT I HELP YOU, BUT I'M GLAD I'M HERE NOW.

IS IT *WEIRD* THAT I THINK I'M ABOUT TO PUNCH MY BEST FRIEND IN THE FACE?

NOPE! IT'S WHAT WE DO.

REALLY NOT SURE, HOW SUN AND SABRINA DO IT.

PUH-LEEZE. THOSE TWO FIGHT MORE THAN ANYONE.

DING DING

5:00

MOLINE
MORRISON

ROUND 1

4:22
Moline
Morrison

LOTS OF FURIOUS ACTION FROM TWO WORLD-CLASS ATHLETES.

3:39
Moline
Morrison

MERCY'S GOING FOR A *TRIANGLE!*

I DON'T THINK KRYSTIN'S IN ANY DANGER.

I THINK SHE'S IN DANGER!

0:01
Moline
Mor...

DING DING

NICE ROUND, DEF TECH.

UM, YEAH. YOU TOO.

GREAT ROUND, BUT I'M GUESSING THE JUDGES FAVORED MERCY THIS ROUND.

THEN KRYSTIN BETTER NOT LET IT GO TO DECISION!

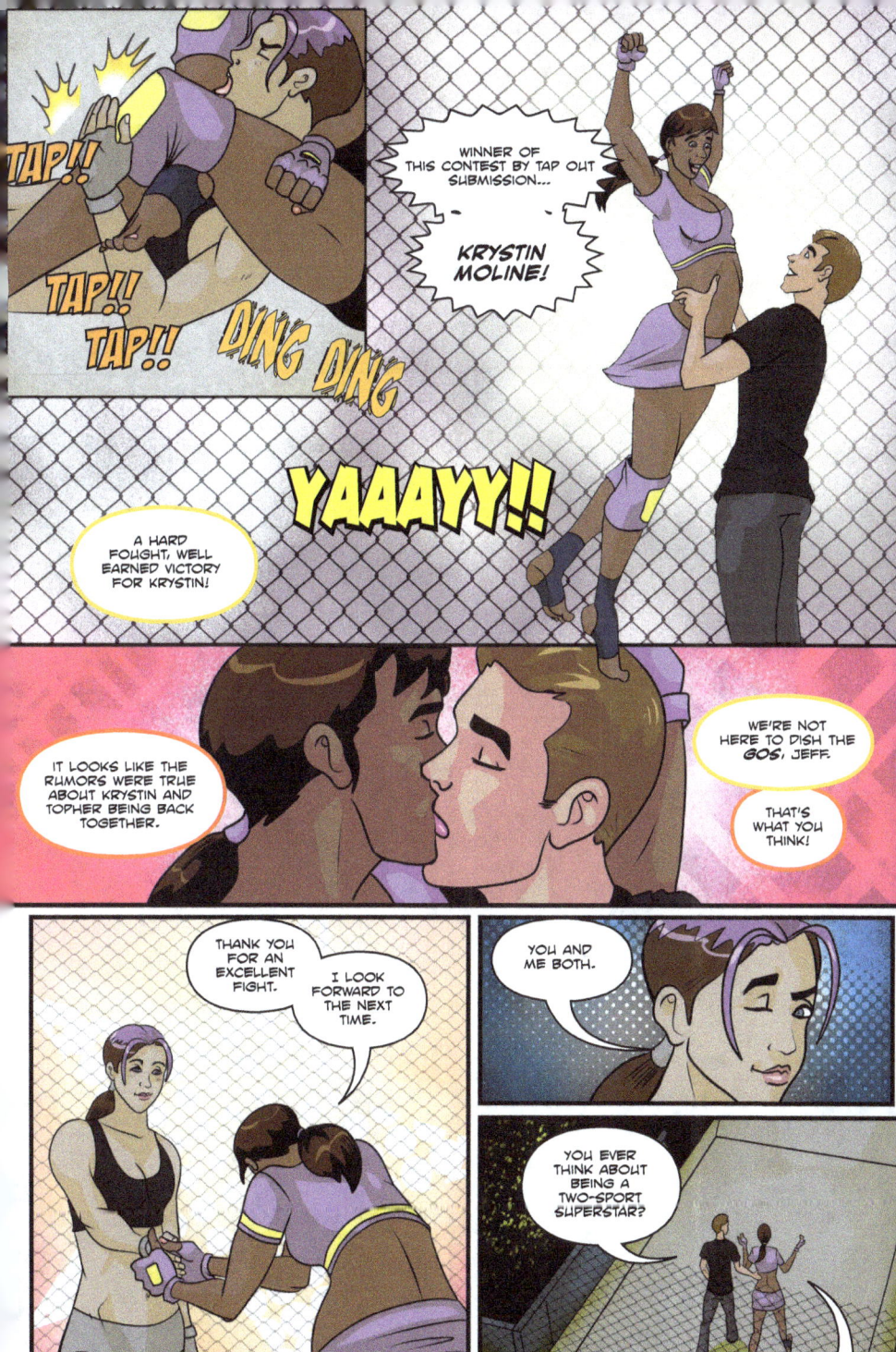

BLACK WIDOW VS. SUN WONG LIL DRAGON

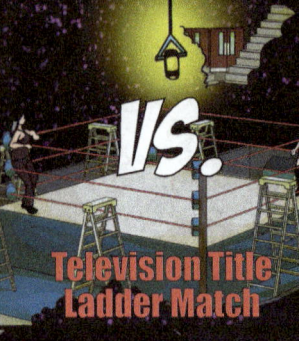

Television Title
Ladder Match

I'M NOT SURE HOW SUN THINKS SHE HAS A CHANCE AGAINST SOMEONE 4X HER SIZE, DAWN.

THERE'S A RUMOR THAT *SUN* AND *BLACK WIDOW* WORKED *TOGETHER* TO TAKE *VICTORIA* OUT IN THE PARKING GARAGE.

I WOULDN'T PUT IT PAST EITHER OF THEM.

THAT'S HOW BAD BOTH LADIES WANT THIS MATCH.

TELL YOU WHAT. I'LL *LET* YOU LEAVE AFTER THIS ONE THING.

SLAP!!

SUN WONG WASTES NO TIME STARTING THE MIND GAMES.

DING DING

YOU'RE DEAD!

YAAAYY!!

SUN POSSESS PRETERNATURAL SPEED.

GET OVER HERE, YOU LITTLE—

MIND GAMES ARE GREAT UNTIL YOU'VE GOT TO BACK THEM UP AGAINST SOMEONE LIKE BLACK WIDOW.

SUN MIGHT BE ENVYING VICTORIA BUCKINGHAM RIGHT ABOUT NOW.
TRAMPLE!
SLAP
GROAN!
STAY DOWN, SHORTY.
THIS MATCH HAS TAKEN A TOLL ON BOTH OF THESE WOMEN.
LET'S GO, SUN!!
LET'S GO, SUN!!
LET'S GO, SUN!!
HAVE YOU HEARD THE GOOD NEWS?
HUH? WHAT ARE YOU-?
YAAAYY!!
I WASN'T WASTING MY TIME WHEN I PRACTICED THE FIGURE FOUR THROUGH THE RUNGS OF A LADDER.
OH! AH! DAMMIT!
BWAHAHAHA!
BUT SUN IS DOWNRIGHT SUDDEN WITH HER OFFENSE. STRAIGHT OUTTA NOWHERE!

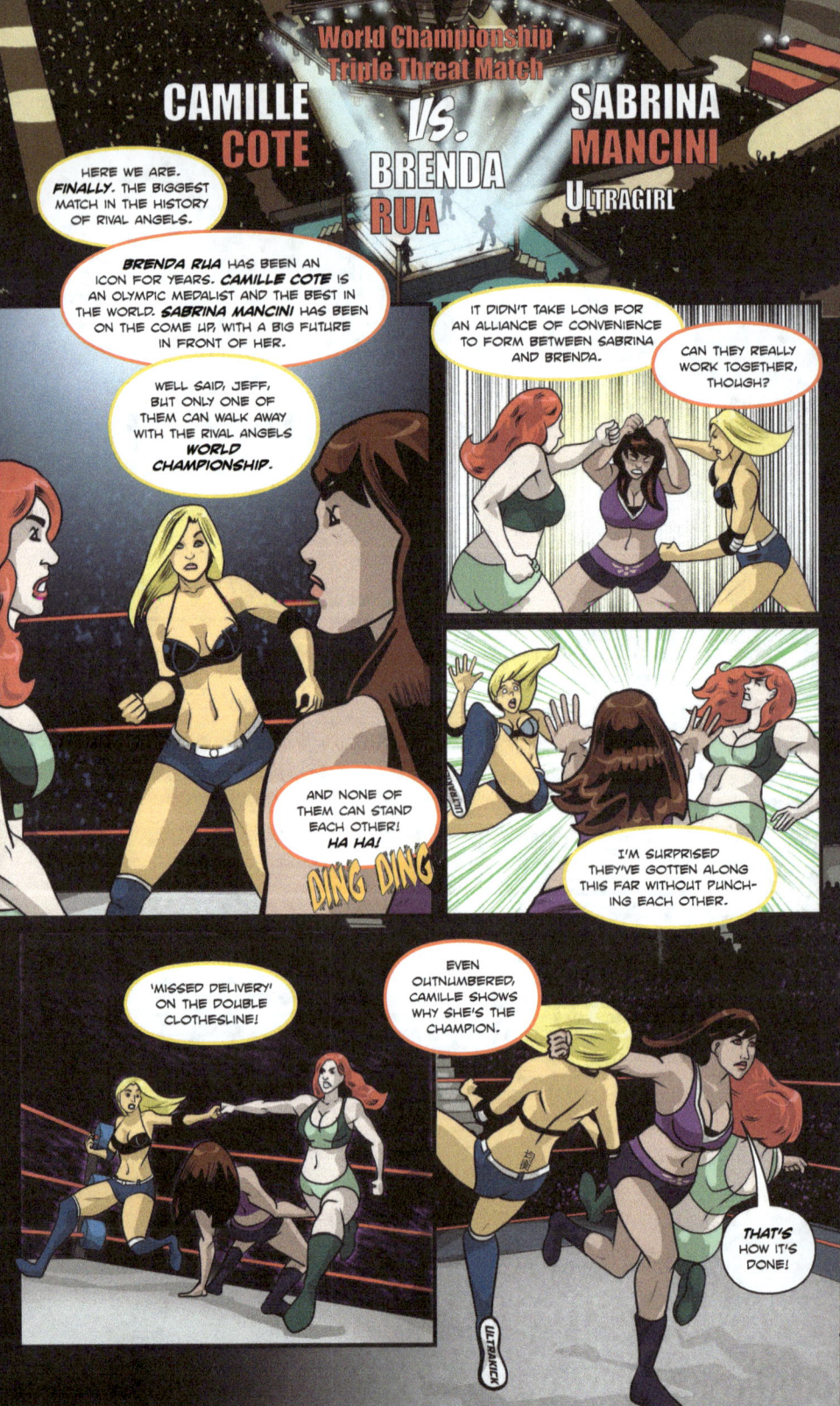

TWO OF THE STRONGEST COMPETITORS ON THE ROSTER LOCKING HORNS.
IT'S LIKE THOR VS. THE HULK!
SABRINA MAY HAVE BEEN BETTER SUITED NOT JOINING THE TEST OF STRENGTH.
SHE LET HER PRIDE GET IN THE WAY.
SA-BRIN-A!
SA-BRIN-A!
YAH!
ULTRAKICK
ULTRAKICK
AND NOW SHE'S GOING FOR A RIDE!
UNEXPECTED TEAMWORK FROM CAMILLE AND BRENDA!
HAS HELL FROZEN OVER?
WHAM!!
GROAN!
JUST A LIGHT FROST.
IT'S A WAR OF ATTRITION! SOMETHING'S GOTTA GIVE, RIGHT?

?
BRAK!
AMAZING AND INNOVATIVE OFFENSE BY CAMILLE COTE!
1....
2...
KICKOUT AT TWO!
MISTAKE BY THE CHAMP. EVERYONE KNOWS THAT SABRINA'S HEAD IS HARDER THAN COMMON CORE MATH.
THE WORLD CHAMPION JUST WENT FROM A PINFALL ATTEMPT TO LOCKING ON A SUBMISSION.
CAMILLE'S VERSATILITY IS UNPARALLELED.
AGH!
KIND OF LIKE SABRINA'S TENACITY!
WHAT GOES OUT FIRST, DAWN, CAMILLE'S LIGHTS OR BRENDA'S BACK?!
YAAAYY!!

BRENDA IS SETTING UP HER OWN INNOVATIVE OFFENSE.

TWO FOR ONE SPECIAL!

KRASH

THUNK

1....

2...

WHERE DO YOU THINK YOU'RE GOING, 'CHAMP?!

GREAT RING AWARENESS BY THE CHAMPION.

KICKOUT!

MAYBE SHE SHOULD HAVE TRIED TO PIN SABRINA.

CAMILLE IS STILL CLEARING THE COBWEBS.

AND BRENDA IS READY TO DROP THE HAMMER ON HER!

UL-TRA-GIRL

UL-TRA-GIRL

HOLY SHI-

UL-TRA-GIRL

ULTRAGIRL FLIES WITH AN INSIDE TO OUTSIDE HURRICANRANA!

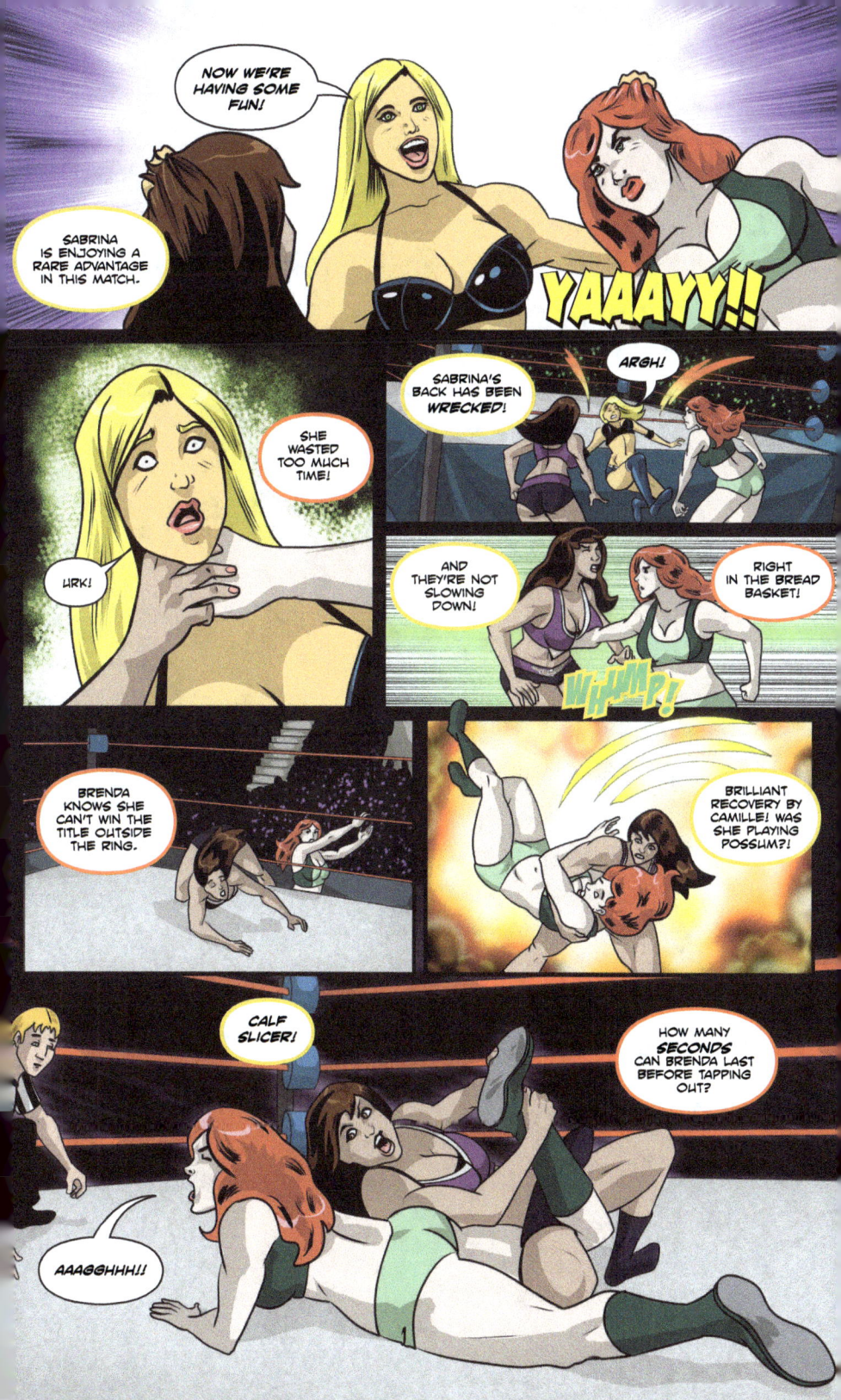

Here we are at the end of things. **Sabrina wins!!** I know a lot of you may have guessed the ending, but I hope I was able to surprise some of you with how she did it. Failing that, I hope you at least had a good time reading it.

This is basically the end I had came up with ten years ago and I'm thrilled to get Rival Angels to this finish. On behalf of Rival Angels, the Upstarts and everyone in-between…

THANK YOU.

The time has come to wrap up the Upstarts story and as it happens, I have other stories to tell. I hope you'll like them too. I won't be straying too far from wrestling art. I owe many pages of women's wrestling to a few fine patrons who have supported me. I hope to share them with you, too, with their permission, of course.

In the summer of 2007, I had come across a new show on the Oxygen network, *Fight Girls*. In the spirit of the UFC's *Ultimate Fighter*, this was a reality TV show where several ladies were chosen to live and train together, ultimately fighting each other to be the winner. Some notable peeps involved were Felice Herring, Michelle Waterson, and Gina Carrano. I was amazed to see something like this on a channel catered towards true crime and women. We've come a long way in 10 years.

There were no wrestling comics, and this show inspired me that there ought to be. Little did I know that Mike Kingston was putting Headlocked out at about this same time. Seems mark minds think alike, and please give Headlocked a try if you haven't. You'll be happy that you did.

The story about 4 sassy girls forced to room together only to discover that their biggest battles would be with each other outside the ring came together very quickly. The hard part was distributing it, but this rather novel approach of 'webcomics' was taking off and I thought I'd give it a try. I wrote the first 20 pages in a Saturday afternoon while waiting for the last Harry Potter book to arrive in the mail. I spent 6 months getting the first 33 pages together, before posting anything online. I wanted a buffer and that buffer got eaten up pretty quickly, but I was always able to stay ahead and deliver without missing an update. 10 years! Of course, I had help along the way.

Back in 2007, webcomics were still pretty new, especially 'giving' things away for free on the internet. Print was king, but I did not find the industry to be very supportive or inviting. When I asked a guy how he did a color technique, he said he'd tell me if I gave him my left nut. Local guys would tell me about shows after they passed asking, 'oh you wanted to be a part of that? Yeah, it was great.' The whole scene was very pessimistic and downright cynical. I was also under the impression that I was done making 'best friends.'

On December 2nd, I posted the first page of Rival Angels on Drunkduck (you can still see it here!) and I was happily surprised to get responses right way. It was weird to get that kind of feedback and support. I posted it early to test-drive it a bit, see if there was anything to iron out for the official launch on my own website, December 30th, 2007.

After the first 33 pages, I brought the 4-way Rookie Rumble which was about 35 pages. What can I say, I wanted a comic about wrestling. I decided that if there wasn't an audience for this, I would hang it up, but there was. After the early success, I decided to take it to the first season and if the interest failed, I'd wrap it up. There was interest and so for another 10 years I brought you the adventures of Sabrina, her BFF Sun and her roommates Krystin and Brooke.

On Drunkduck I met some people like Amy and Kay King, DAJB, Barb Jacobs, Amanda and Jess, Scott Sava, Rose Loughran, Kurt Sasso, and many more that deserve to be listed. However, the two people that I met there that changed the course of both my life and Rival Angels are Trevor Mueller and Lora Innes. They both were on Drunkduck with @$$hole and The Dreamer respectively and they were both very encouraging and supportive, very much a contrast to what I had experienced locally and in Print circles. Trevor and I did a LOT of conventions together trying to figure out comic conventions, anime conventions and everything in-between. We went to the 3rd or 4th Anime Milwaukee which was held in the hallways of the UWM campus building. We've been guests of the show for the last several years and it was one of our favorite shows to do.

To this day I'm always trying to improve and I'd still been gun shy about asking other artists about their process, wanting to keep my nuts to myself, if not for Lora. I took a chance and asked her about what kind of Lead Holder (pencil) she used. She was very happy to share! Lora has always been an incredible artist and I've always looked up to her as an artist, but also as an terrific person and an amazing friend. I'm so glad I asked. She's like my brainy little sister whose always right.

Trevor, Mike and Lora are some of my best friends and I have Rival Angels to thank for that and will always be forever grateful.

2008 saw my first Wizard World with Rival Angels and I knew that Trevor and Lora were going to be there. I reached out to Lora to see if she'd like to split a table. She agreed, and I got to spend the weekend with her and her amazing husband, Mike. With Trevor's table nearby, it was truly a wonderful weekend of talking comics, optimism and all around having fun. I also got to meet Dave Reynolds and Dave Rodriguez who were doing a really fun comic, Shadowgirls.

2009 allowed Trevor and I to widen our net a bit and looked at this show in Columbus called, Mid-Ohio Con. It just so happens that Lora and Mike lived in Columbus and when they heard that we were coming, they offered us a place to stay. Being from Milwaukee, I was immediately suspicious. Why would they want to help us? And comic peeps to boot! I had learned locally that there would be no support, and that someone else's success was your failure, So what gives? Eventually Mike reasoned that we'd save a lot of money crashing at their place rather than getting a hotel. This was the thing to make me give in and I'm so glad that he appealed to my frugality. I also met Thom, Paul, Bryan and Dirk at this show, again all of whom were very inviting and supportive. Amazing people whom I'm thrilled to call my friends.

Soon after that, I discovered an all-women's indy show outside of Chicago called SHIMMER, a superb organization ran by Dave Prazak, who has always been supportive of Rival Angels. He let me distribute Rival Angels mini-comics and did I ever find my audience, as well as several more friends in Jim, Brian, Darryl, Randy, Chris, Joe and of course, the wonderful and talented Cheerleader December.

More people that have enriched my life are John and Mallory, Sean and Sara, Russell, Horton, Wallace and so many more.

From there to here, Rival Angels opened so many doors. It got me my last two jobs. It has afforded me to travel around the country, and helped me become a better artist and storyteller.

From an early time, I referred to Rival Angels as the '#1 Wrestling Comic,' and for the most part it was true because there really weren't any others. I will say that I've always been a little uneasy with that after James Hornsby started Botched Spot. He does a fabulous wrestling webcomic, surely deserving the #1 wrestling webcomic moniker. If you haven't checked out his work, you need to. Botched Spot is sharp, funny and insightful.

I want to thank the people who have helped me along the way. Veronica Rosado who colored those first 33 pages, and Dan Head for helping me with the early script. His input has always been invaluable. Jules Rivera with some emergency colors when I was overseas, and came through wonderfully and who has the distinction of working on Rival Angels and Headlocked. Pretty cool, if you ask me. My flatters Mabel Lim and Aaron Daly who have been with me forever. Aaron, I hope we get to share a drink the next time I'm in town. Kay King, (who along with her sister did an amazing comic, .031) came on late with the regular colors and has killed it. She raised the game of Rival Angels exponentially. Cale who has come through with dozens of images of story when I put out the call for readers for the winter break, and who has created his own amazing characters like Lucy the Crusher. Dave Reynolds needs special attention for the pages and pages of material that he's done, as well as masterfully coloring pages when I needed them. Dave's always had my back and I'm so appreciative that he's here.

I want to thank Kristen Perry for spending so much time helping me be a better artist and for saying, 'It's never too late to be the artist you want to be.' I'll never forget that. In a roundabout way, she helped me get over anxiety of meeting someone you look up to. In 2007 at Wizard World, I had a chance to meet her, but I bitched out. Too nervous! After all of these years, I hope to correct that error. She's been more influential on my work than she could know.

I want to thank Trevor for always being so supportive and always having my back. Long road trips to here and there were always well spent together and I couldn't think of a better person to take the webcomics plunge with. You make me want to be a better friend.

I want to thank Lora for being my webcomics BFF, and for also spending so much time helping me be a better artist. I'm still not there, but I'm miles closer because of you. Thanks for answering my question about Lead Holders. I don't know that I have the words for thanking someone for being such a wonderful friend, but if I did, they'd be spent on you and Mike. Thanks for letting me be a part of your life, and being a part of mine. You make me want to be a better friend.

You guys don't hear a lot about Justin Riley, and I don't know if that's been by design or not. Justin is one of my oldest friends and has helped me with writing chores on every single Rival Angels book. Actually, every single page of Rival Angels. If you laughed at something; it was probably something he came up with. If something was profound or made you think; he had a hand in it. Rival Angels is better because of you and thank you for that. Thank you for letting me take up your Friday nights with post-its, notes and black foam core. Thanks for always being my friend. Thanks for treating Sun as yours, because she always will be.

It has been my experience that your family will not be as supportive in your endeavors as you might like for whatever reason. Plenty of family have reminded me that I could draw other things. Plenty of people have asked, 'what does your wife think of this?' They are always surprised when Tracie would let them know in no uncertain terms that she loves Rival Angels. I cannot undersell the support that I've received from my wife all of these years. I just don't think I'd have it in me to keep doing something that wasn't supported by her. I have friends who didn't have that support in their passion, and it blew my mind, but never surprised me when they fell short. Rival Angels was a passion project but the one reader I always pictured was her, and she would let me know if I hit the mark or needed to hit the literal or proverbial drawing board. Thank you for helping me with Rival Angels. The beginning, in-between and getting her to the finish line. It's your victory as much as mine and I know you'll be with me by my side on the next projects that come along and take time away from us. I love you always.

Rival Angels is dedicated to friends and friends who become family.

No amount of thanks will be enough to you, dear reader, but with the most sincere, from the bottom of my heart, thank you very much. Your faith and support have been immeasurable and I will never forget it. I hope you like what I have next. Thank you for reading all of this and as it turns out….there IS just a little bit more of Sabrina, Sun, Krystin and Brooke. Come back next Wednesday at the usual time, eh?

Thanks!

Alan Evans
Rival Angels
Updated for 10 years without missing an update,
though I'm ready for a break.

McGillicutty's

IT'S BEEN A COUPLE OF MONTHS SINCE YOU AND *JAKE* MOVED IN TOGETHER. HOW IS LIFE LIVING WITH A BOY?

HE LEAVES THE *SEAT* DOWN. IT'S LIKE A FAIRY TALE.

I CAN'T BELIEVE HE CAN SLEEP THROUGH YOUR SNORING.

WE DON'T KNOW THAT HE CAN. HE MIGHT BE TOO SCARED TO TELL HER.

TOPHER DOESN'T EVEN HIT THE *BOWL*, LET ALONE PUT THE SEAT DOWN.

THINGS HAVE BEEN OUT OF CONTROL BUSY SINCE THE HEAVEN AND HELL PAY-PER-VIEW.

WHAT DO *YOU GUYS* THINK WILL HAPPEN NEXT?

XTREME
MOLINE - TAYLOR

WOW, WHAT DID WE DO?

WE DID A THING!

WE MEET WITH THE STAFF IN AN HOUR.

YOU READY?

YEAH.

YOU DIDN'T START *MAIN EVENTING* RIVAL ANGELS UNTIL YOU STARTED WINNING *CAGE* FIGHTS.

IT'S OKAY TO LEAN INTO THAT.

6 MONTHS, PRO WRESTLING. 6 MONTHS, MMA. WHAT COULD GO WRONG WITH THAT?

YOU'RE GOING TO BE GREAT.

WE GOT AN HOUR, HUH?

XTREME
MOLINE - TAYLOR

WE HAVE ENOUGH FOR *FANTASY SETTING #33* IN THE OCTAGON.

I *AM* WEARING MY LAP DANCE PANTS.

APHRODITE
YAAAYY!!
WEL-COME BACK!
WEL-COME BACK!
WEL-COME BACK!
BROOKE LENNOX IS THE NEW GM OF RIVAL ANGELS!
THE DOUBLE D GODDESS IS BACK!
RIVAL ANGELS RATINGS ARE GREAT, BUT IF YOU WANT RECORD-SETTING YOU HAVE TO GO THE EXTRA MILE.
WITH 'GIRAFFECANE 4' ALL WRAPPED UP, THE GODDESS IS BACK AS YOUR NEW GM!
I PROMISE YOU ALL TWO THINGS. I PROMISE TO BE FAIR. MORE IMPORTANTLY I PROMISE TO BE HOT!
NOW, DID YOU KNOW THERE'S ONE THING THAT MIGHT BE HOTTER THAN ME IN THIS RING?
CAN YOU SAY UPSTARTS REUNION?
CAN YOU SCREAM IT?!
YAAAYY!!

Training Day by Cale Ranots

From Wikipedia...

Catch wrestling is a classical hybrid grappling style that was developed in Britain circa 1870 by J. G. Chambers, then later refined and popularised by the wrestlers of travelling funfairs who developed their own submission holds, or "hooks", into their wrestling to increase their effectiveness against their opponents.

I think it was Josh Barnett who once explained that, although many of the submission techniques are similar to Ju-Jitsu (he was specifically comparing to Brazilian Ju-Jitsu), there was a key philosophical difference.

Barnett explained that BJJ practitioners are "trappers" - they set you up by leaving you with what you think is an opening, only to sucker and finish you when you go for it.

On the other hand, catch wrestlers are "hunters" - they aren't waiting for you to fall in a trap; rather they are actively looking for something to grab a hold of so they can twist, crank, or squeeze it.

These two grapplers have different motivations. They both want to develop and practise their catch techniques.
They've decided to do this in a cage rather than a ring or open mat...

Wonder how this is going to go down?

Lucy is working her arm around the back of Sabrina's head. Maybe she's still warming up or maybe she's just careless. No matter, Lucy telegraphs her hip, and Sabrina sees the attempted throw coming from a long way away.

Instead it's Sabrina who makes the first move. Letting go of the back of Lucy's head, Sabrina shoots her left arm down over her opponent's right shoulder at the same time as she spins away, finally using her right hand to grab Lucy's right wrist.

The Waki Gatame arm bar as a takedown technique is banned in a lot of competitions because of how dangerously easy it is to wreck your opponent's arm before they can tap safely. Sabrina is fairly careful here, but Lucy still needs to move fast to avoid the plaster.

Face down onto the mat that is. Pinned, there's nothing left but the tap out.

"That was kind of a dick move. Are we working out or are you trying to hurt someone? "

"Ok... I'll be more careful..."

There are a few ways you can lose a wrestling match. Obviously your opponent can make you tap out. That's popular in some circles.

But the classic 1, 2, and 3 is also a tried and tested method.

Lucy reckons she's going to settle Sabrina down a bit. With her legs tied up like this, Sabrina is not getting off her back any time just yet.

Sabrina refuses to tap out, so Lucy moves to something else.

Lucy is pretty blown away shortly thereafter – Sabrina doesn't just tough this out, she escapes!

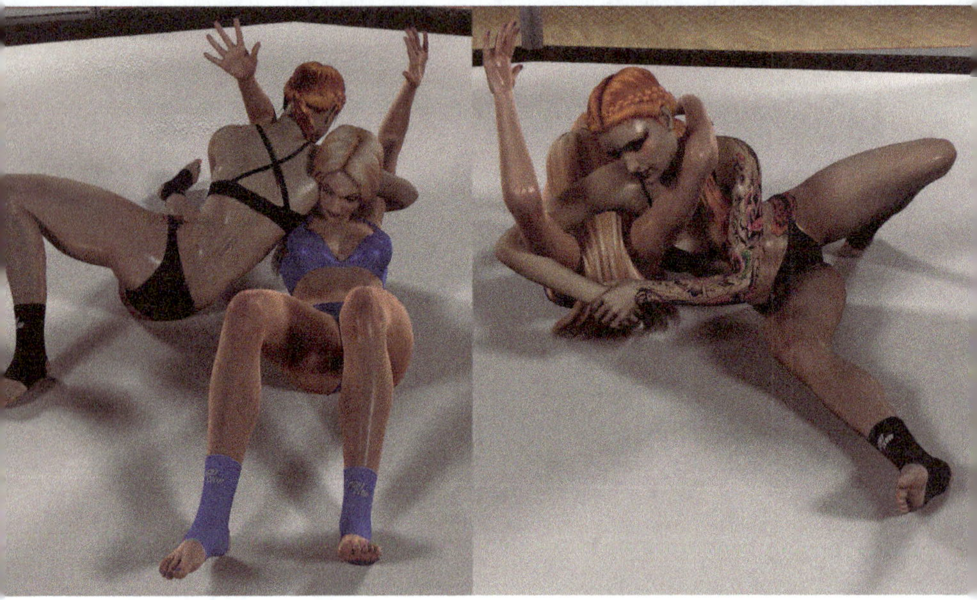

In the ensuing scramble Lucy ends up north/south on the mat with Sabrina.

Lucy knows what a toe hold looks like and how to apply them. She also knows when someone else has got one locked down tighter than the proverbial.

Lucy manages to spin and relieve the pressure once. Sabrina spins with and hangs on.

Tap out number two for Sabrina (for those keeping score).

Lucy has dropped a couple of falls, time to try working from top position again. Sabrina's guard is pretty good, but maybe Lucy can hold her shoulder blades down for a three count.

Or maybe not?

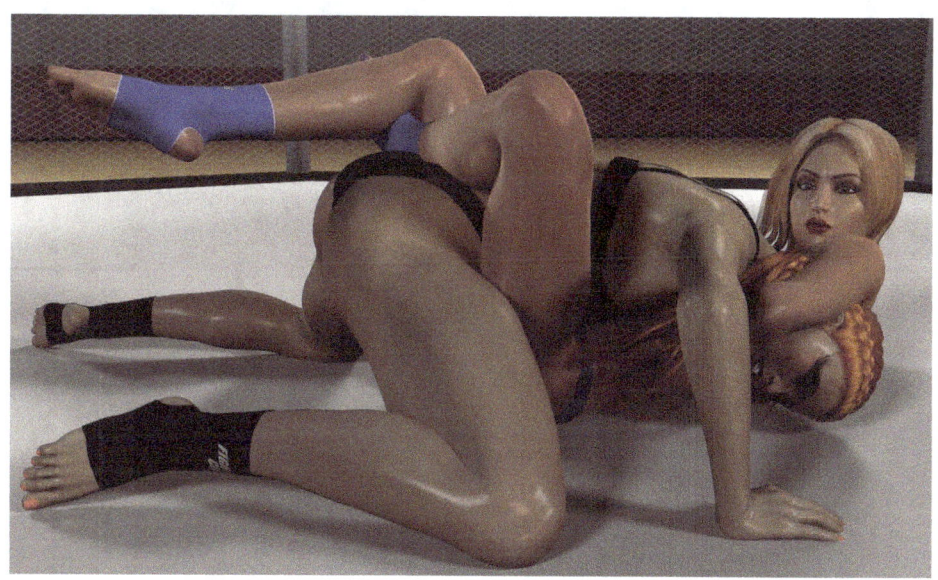

One of these again? Someone is getting trampled today!

Let's go back to trying from top position again. Sabrina has a signature move from this position. Lucy knows that. Should have known that? Well – Lucy knows that now.

Ok, Lucy knows the score now. She's come here to train. Sabrina is on a *mission*.

Lucy has two choices. She can keep getting "trained" (more on that later) or...

Sabrina is trying to get ready for some big matches. If Lucy wants to help her get ready, then she needs to lift her own game.

Well, all right then.

Lucy moves faster than she had before today, getting both of Sabrina's legs.

Lift and drop onto her back. Sabrina makes what may be her first mistake; fearing the pin, she gives up her back. Lucy has decided she wants to put Sabrina on her back again...

Done, but still moving patiently. Lucy holds mount. She isn't forcing the pin that hard. At least not yet.

Rather, Lucy seems to be holding position and setting for something else.

Well, that's not very elegant.

Sabrina is expending a lot of energy right now...

Lucy shoots herself up slightly, then down.

Sabrina stays calm, for about 15 seconds. Right now though, she is struggling mightily.

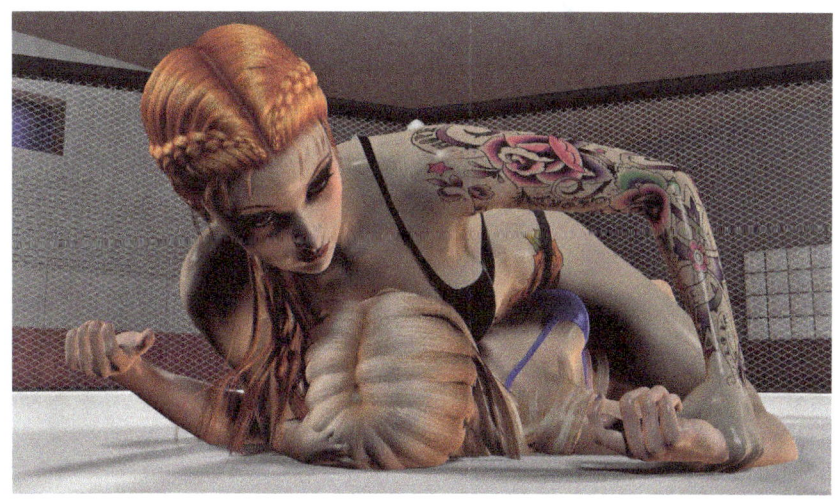

"What the? What are you doing? I didn't tap out?"

"So you want to get ready for a big match, yeah? Some advice for you. Emotion only helps when your head stays in charge of your heart. Lots of energy is no substitute for a lack of attention and technique."

"Yeah? So?"

"What was I doing 10 second ago, besides suffocating you that is?"

A memory clicks into place...

"You were counting."

"Right! What number did I get to?"

"... Three... You counted three and both my shoulders were down."

...

"*Shit....*"

"Ok then, let's resume...."

Lucy thinks maybe she can back off a little bit now.

That was incorrect...

Now, Lucy is bringing her own emotional energy along as well. She doesn't want to hurt anyone, so maybe something else?

Sabrina is hanging tough. Really tough. Lucy isn't letting go, transitioning from one arm to a full RNC and body lock.

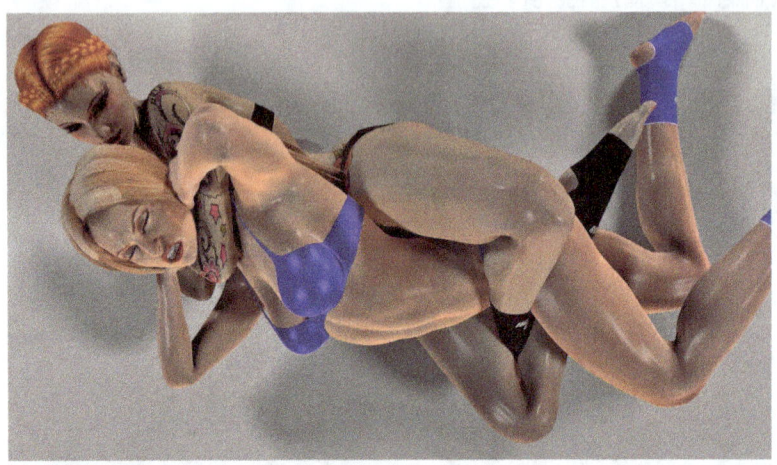

Lucy is impressed. Sabrina is fighting this one. Face down isn't that great an improvement though.

But now Sabrina gets back to all fours... What the...?

Sabrina crawls to the chain link. That's ok, there's no rope break... But... Holy crap! Sabrina doesn't just power back to her feet! Somehow, she finds a way to twist suddenly and... Sabrina is out of the sleeper!

At least Lucy still has full guard... What happens next? Is Sabrina going for a pin from here or something else? Will Lucy get advantage back?

Nope! Sabrina stalls for a few moments getting her composure back, but with an almost feral energy she gets the Ezekiel choke for the fall herself!

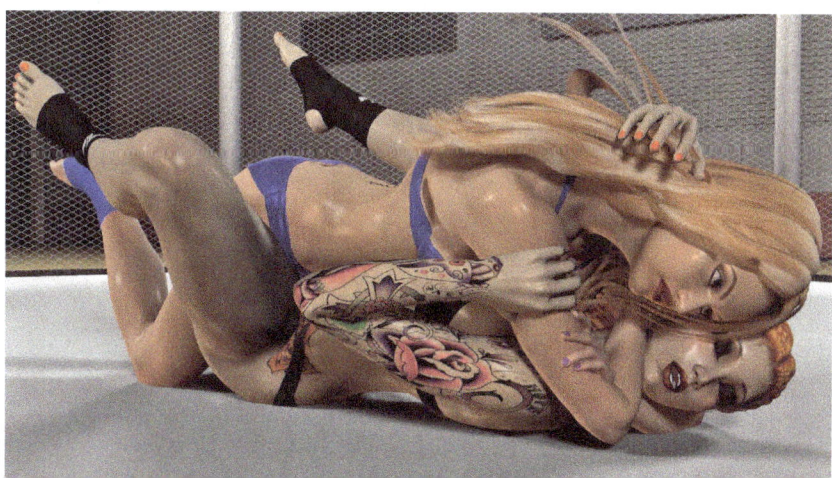

Lucy has just about had enough. Channelling her inner mongrel, she puts Sabrina on her back again, working the pin. Sabrina extends her arm for balance to push up and keep her shoulders up.

Lucy sees that and, with exactly the speed you'd expect from a serious amateur wrestler, grabs hold of that extended arm, then starts cranking. And now Sabrina is hurting and making noise.

So Lucy lets go.

"What is it this time?"

"You're still fighting stupid. I had you and I had your arm – deep. You weren't working your way out; you were just trying to brute force it. I know who you're training for. If they get you like that and you don't work smart, what do you think is going to happen to your arm? Or do you think it's good prep if I put you in plaster myself?"

"...Shit..."

"C'mon. Get your head into this and keep it there. Ready to go again?"

"Yeah..."

Lucy gets another choke hold; if anything she locks down even tighter this time.

Sabrina fights it again – maybe even harder than before. This time it's not enough. Stamina matters – has Sabrina been going too hard too fast?

Sabrina wakes up – Lucy insists Sabrina takes her time to recover. Sabrina is tired, and by the time she realises the sweep was a fake it's too late for her to roll out of the Omoplata.

But still Sabrina is refusing to tap. Lucy shakes her head... In fairness, Sabrina is working and Lucy isn't cranking the shoulder that hard. Sabrina lifts her head up, exposing her neck. Lucy gets a different idea...

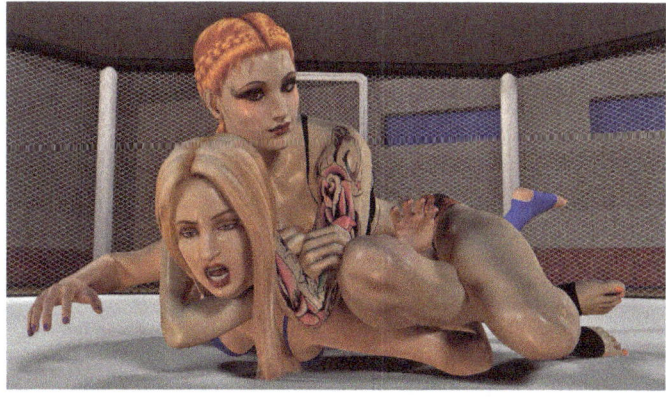

Sabrina taps, but after Lucy asks if she's done the reaction is pretty vehement. Sabrina knows that, when it matters, you have to find a way to keep going. She's not done yet, she insists.

But after falling into guard again, she does give up her first legit tap out.

Back on their feet, Lucy mixes things up. They lock up standing. Even if Sabrina wasn't tired, there's still a good chance she's going to get bulled to the fence. Once she's on the fence? Lucy sets her base and leans in. Sabrina feels like she's pinned against the chain link by a phone pole.

Pushing and shoving, Sabrina thinks she can get an out, reaching her left arm across the back of Lucy's neck. At the same time she slips Lucy's underhook on the right. Except that just went very badly wrong when Lucy closes the triangle in a standing position.

Desperate, Sabrina shoves and twists. She pushes up. She drops with all her weight.

She's still pinned between chain link and a phone pole.

When she wakes up, Lucy apologises. "Sorry – didn't mean to let you drop that hard."

Old school – when you're on fumes, sometimes the simplest stuff is the hardest to break.

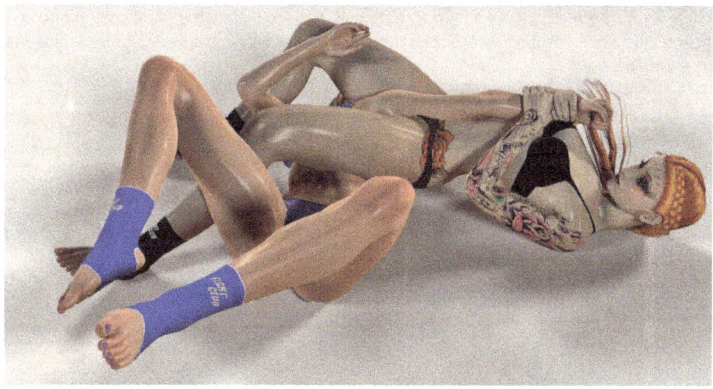

But not done yet. Somewhere Sabrina finds a bit more gas. Lucy picked the wrong time to get complacent...

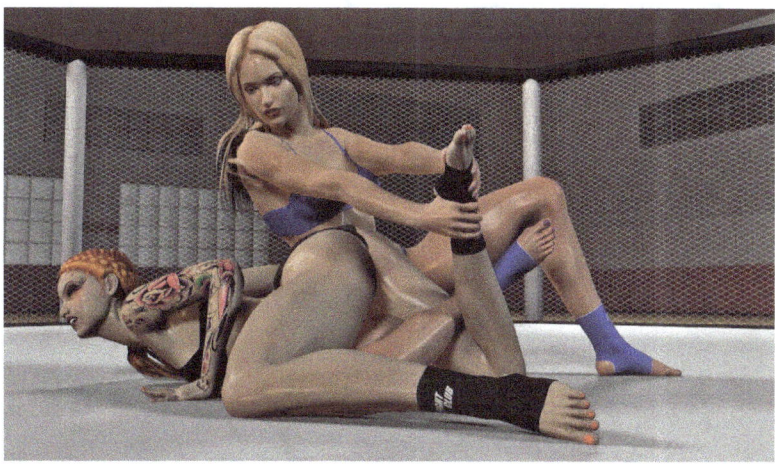

Lucy has gotten a bit gassed herself, and now Sabrina has a second wind. This is setting up to something, Lucy knows she needs to change this up fast.

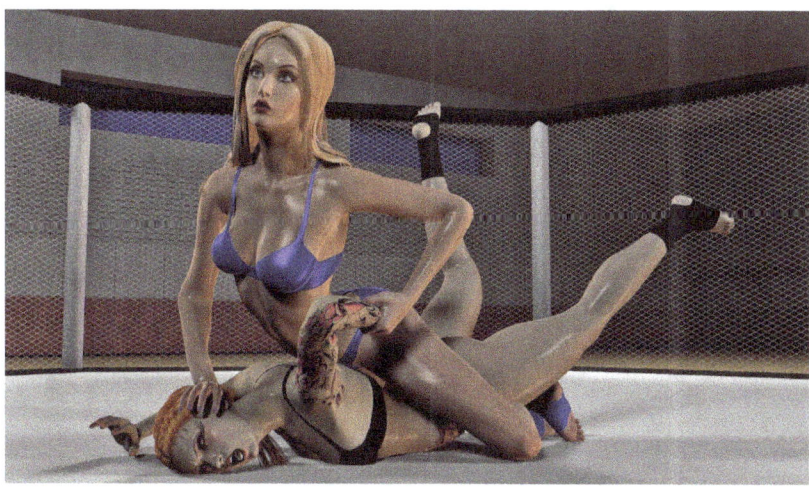

The Crusher uses that famed lower body strength to twist and buck. It's harder to keep your technique clean when you're tired. Normally when you brute strength it, that's an act of desperation and often doesn't work. Lucy gets back to top – hey it worked! Except now she's gagging air into her lungs and, that tired, makes a more serious mistake.

Lucy rolls again. Sabrina holds on and rolls with. This time Lucy is the one who waits too long to tap.

Sabrina offers Lucy the breather. Lucy takes it. This time she's more careful and holds her own energy and stamina more tightly. And when she locks in the bicep slicer, that's pretty tight also.

So this is the difference. Lucy has found a little bit and knows how to ration it. Sabrina's got nothing left. Still she holds, and as long as she's working Lucy doesn't twist all the way. Finally Sabrina knows she's caught...

"Ah fuck..." This time she taps.

Sabrina gets top. Lucy paces, Sabrina reaches. Too far and too careless.

Still – that heart. Even Lucy is surprised.

This time Lucy doesn't ask, she offers. "I need a shower and a beer. How about it?"

It seems someone agrees.

Acknowledgements

Special thanks to the Rival Angels readers!

Kickstarter Sponsors and Patrons

Jim Payne
KONSTANTINE
Brian Bishop
$tev
Bruce S. Fein
J. B. Garner
Rohan Graetz

Ring Crew

To those that listen,
indulge, build up and support.

Aaron
Mabel
Kay
Dave
Lora
Justin
Tracie

www.ingramcontent.com/pod-product-compliance
Lightning Source LLC
Chambersburg PA
CBHW071119100726
47908CB00008B/2426